# Rough Crossing

## by Tom Stoppard

Freely adapted from
Ferenc Molnar's
*Play at the Castle*

A SAMUEL FRENCH ACTING EDITION

# SAMUEL FRENCH

FOUNDED 1830

New York Hollywood London Toronto

SAMUELFRENCH.COM

A COPY OF THE PIANO MUSIC FOR THE SONGS ARE ENTR'ACTE IS AVAILABLE FOR PURCHASE.

ISBN   978-0-573-66206-5      Printed   in   U.S.A.      #20102

### MUSIC USE NOTE

Licensees are solely responsible for obtaining formal written permission from copyright owners to use copyrighted music in the performance of this play and are strongly cautioned to do so. If no such permission is obtained by the licensee, then the licensee must use only original music that the licensee owns and controls. Licensees are solely responsible and liable for all music clearances and shall indemnify the copyright owners of the play and their licensing agent, Samuel French, Inc., against any costs, expenses, losses and liabilities arising from the use of music by licensees.

### IMPORTANT BILLING AND CREDIT REQUIREMENTS

All producers of *ROUGH CROSSING must* give credit to the Author of the Play in all programs distributed in connection with performances of the Play, and in all instances in which the title of the Play appears for the purposes of advertising, publicizing or otherwise exploiting the Play and/or a production. The name of the Author *must* appear on a separate line on which no other name appears, immediately following the title and *must* appear in size of type not less than fifty percent of the size of the title type.

# CHARACTERS

TURAI.... *Playwright and collaborator with Gal, of middle age*

GAL ... *Playwright and collaborator with Turai, of middle age*

ADAM..................... *A young composer, aged 25*

NATASHA ................. *An actress, aged 35 to 40*

IVOR ...................... *An actor, aged 45 to 50*

DVORNICHEK ................... *A cabin steward*

The action takes place on board the *SS ITALIAN CASTLE* sailing between Southampton and New York via Cherbourg.

# A NOTE ON THE ACCENTS

Little or nothing hinges on the nationality of the characters. In the original production TURAI and GAL, who retain their names from the Hungarian, spoke virtually without an accent. NATASHA spoke with a Hungarian accent invoking the tradition of English-speaking Continental stars, but this is not a vital matter. More point is made of ADAM's being French, so he spoke with the appropriate accent. IVOR is English. My assumption about DVORNICHEK is that whatever his nationality his English is mysteriously perfect.

# ROUGH CROSSING

## ACT ONE

*The private verandas of the two most expensive suites on the Italian Castle. Turai's veranda is needed more than Natasha's veranda. Entrances on to this little deck are made from upstage through the interior, partly visible, of Turai's sitting room.*

*It is late at night. There is enough moonlight and electric light around to ensure that we are not peering into the gloom.*

*TURAI is standing by the rail.*

*DVORNICHEK approaches from within, balancing a silver tray on one hand, and also balancing himself as though the boat were in a storm.*

*(Later when the boat is in a storm, and when everybody else is staggering about, the boat's movements seem to cancel out DVORNICHEK's so that he is the only person moving around normally.)*

DVORNICHEK. *(Entering)* Here we are, sir! One cognac!
TURAI. Oh ... Thank you.

DVORNICHEK. For those in peril on the sea there's nothing like a large cognac as a steadying influence.

TURAI. You could do with a steadying influence yourself. You'd better put it down.

DVORNICHEK. Thank you, sir. Your health. *(He drinks the cognac.)* And may I say what an honour it is to serve you, sir! *(He stands swaying.)* Quite a swell!

TURAI. *(modestly)* Thank you.

DVORNICHEK. Will there be anything else, sir?

TURAI. Perhaps a cognac.

DVORNICHEK. I recommend it, sir. It calms the waters something wonderful.

TURAI. Thank you ... er ...

DVORNICHEK. Dvornichek, sir.

TURAI. Dvornichek. But surely we're still in harbour.

DVORNICHEK. *(surprised)* Are we, sir? I see no sign of it.

TURAI. It's on the other side of the boat.

DVORNICHEK. By God, you're right. I thought the front end was *that* way, but that's the back end, is it?, and you've got a right-hand-side room.

TURAI. Starboard.

DVORNICHEK. I beg your pardon, sir?

TURAI. Er...

DVORNICHEK. Dvornichek.

TURAI. Dvornichek. So this is your first crossing?

DVORNICHEK. *(impressed)* That's miraculous. I suppose in your line of work you can tell a character at a glance.

TURAI. It's a gift. I take no credit for it. Where was your

last position?

DVORNICHEK. Paris, sir. The George. *(French pronunciation)*

TURAI. Cinq?

DVORNICHEK. No, it's a hotel. I'd be grateful if you didn't mention it to anyone. I told them it was the *Mauretania*. They suspect nothing in the basement.

TURAI. I should try to pick up a few nautical expressions.

DVORNICHEK. That's a very good idea, sir. I shall start immediately.

TURAI. And could you find Mr. Gal for me.

DVORNICHEK. No problem. He went to the telegraph office.

TURAI. Where is that?

DVORNICHEK. On the ... starboard side, sir. Up by the chimneys. I'll be back with your drink in no time.

TURAI. Get one too for Mr. Adam - his cabin is opposite mine on the other side of the boat.

DVORNICHEK. Yes, sir.

TURAI. Port.

DVORNICHEK. Yes, sir. And a cognac.

TURAI. Er...

DVORNICHEK. Dvornichek.

TURAI. Dvornichek. Present my compliments and ask Mr. Adam what he'd like to drink. And, by the way, be patient when you speak with him - he suffers from a nervous disability, in fact a speech impediment, which takes the unusual form of ... *(He sees that ADAM has entered the cabin and is approaching. As ADAM enters the deck:)* Ah, dear boy, how are you! Come out here—

DVORNICHEK. Good evening, sir.

*(Everything stops. ADAM'S nervous disability takes the form of a pause of several seconds before he can embark on a sentence. Once he starts, he speaks perfectly normally without stuttering. One result of this, in certain situations, is that ADAM is always answering the last question but one. Later on in the play, unless otherwise indicated, ADAM always hesitates before embarking on a speech but usually the hesitation is notional.)*

ADAM. *(finally)* Good evening.

DVORNICHEK. Welcome aboard, sir. If there's anything I can do for you don't hesitate to ask. *(pause)*

ADAM. Thank you, I won't.

TURAI. All unpacked? Found a place for everything?

DVORNICHEK. I expect you'd like a drink, sir?

ADAM. Oh, yes, but I haven't brought much with me.

DVORNICHEK. No problem, we've got plenty, you'll be all right with us.

ADAM. No, I don't think I will.

DVORNICHEK. Course you will - I trust your cabin is satisfactory?

TURAI. How did you find your lady love?

ADAM. Most comfortable, thank you.

TURAI. Have you seen her yet?

DVORNICHEK. Are you going to get one in?

ADAM. Not yet, she's still at dinner.

DVORNICHEK. No, I mean a drink. A port, wasn't it?

TURAI. Why don't we wait for her together?

ADAM. No, really, thank you.

DVORNICHEK. We've got a Rebello-Valente 1911, or there's the '24.

ADAM. Thank you, I'd like that very much.

DVORNICHEK. Which?

TURAI. *(Crossly, to DVORNICHEK)* What do you *want?*

DVORNICHEK. Oh, thank you, I'll have a cognac.

ADAM. I don't drink port.

TURAI. We could send word to her table that we're on board.

DVORNICHEK. Forget the port - we've got everything. Just name it.

ADAM. No, I'd like it to be a surprise.

DVORNICHEK. A surprise. Right.

TURAI. Er...

DVORNICHEK. Dvornichek.

TURAI. Dvornichek - go away.

DVORNICHEK. Go away ... right. No problem. *(He goes away. If there are chairs, TURAI and ADAM make themselves comfortable. There is quite a long pause while ADAM struggles into speech.)*

ADAM. Let's not talk if you don't mind because my starting motor is behaving worse than ever no doubt from the excitement of seeing Natsha again and I feel so silly having to choose between on the one hand struggling to resume each time the flow is interrupted and on the other hand gabbling non-stop so as to give an impression of easy conversation which isn't in fact easy when you are trapped like a rat in a runaway train of ever more complicated sentences that shy away from the approaching full stop like a - like a - damn!

TURAI. *(TURAI waves him courteously to silence.)* Like a moth shying at a candle flame. Too boring. At a lepidopterist, then. Too banal. Like a girl shying at her first compliment. Oh, I like that. Like a boy shying at a coconut, no, I've gone too far again. How ironical that tongue-trippery should come in my shape and tripped-uppery in yours. I sound like a leading man, and you look like one, and between us we have to rely on clods like Ivor Fish to present the world with our genius. Oh, hello, Gal, your genius too, of course.

*(This is because GAL has emerged from inside the cabin. He is perhaps not as clothes-conscious as TURAI but has at least an equal dignity. This is not impaired by the fact that he happens to be eating a stick of celery.)*

GAL. There you are, Turai. Good evening, Adam. Any sign of Natasha? Don't reply. And don't listen to Turai. He has no genius. He can write a bit but unfortunately writes a lot. I have no genius either. Economy of expression I have. I have cabled New York.

TURAI. We really would have taken your word for it.

ADAM. No, she's still at dinner.

GAL. I've ordered a cognac.

TURAI. What did you say?

GAL. 'Bring me a cognac.'

TURAI. This was the cable to New York?

GAL. You have become confused. We have an excellent cabin steward. I forget his name. I asked him to bring me a cognac. The cable to New York was another thing altogether: 'Safely embarked *SS Italian Castle,* arriving Sunday with new ending, don't worry.' I thought it best not to mention the new beginning.

TURAI. What's wrong with the beginning?

GAL. Won't do. Curtain up. Chaps talking. Who are they? We don't know. They're talking about something they evidently know all about and we know nothing about. Then another chap. Who is he? They know so they won't tell us. Five minutes have gone by. Everything must fall into place or we'll stop caring. They mention a woman. Who is she? We don't know. They know so they won't tell us. So it goes.

TURAI. *The Merchant of Venice* begins like that.

GAL. There you are, you see. Won't do.

TURAI. What do you suggest?

GAL. Introduce a character part, on board the boat but outside the main story; comes in at the beginning and recognizes *everybody*, knows exactly what they are up to and fills in the whole jigsaw with one speech. He could be an Irish policeman called Murphy.

TURAI. Yes ... I don't know, though ... an Irish policeman called Murphy right at the beginning of *The Merchant of Venice*.

GAL. I'm not talking about *The Merchant of Venice*.

TURAI. Oh, I see. But why should the policeman *do* such a thing?

GAL. Why shouldn't he?

TURAI. And why is he Irish?

GAL. I had a reason for that but I've forgotten what it was.

TURAI. And what is an Irish policeman doing on the boat anyway?

GAL. Emigrating.

TURAI. But it's a round-the-world cruise.

GAL. *That's* what it was.

TURAI. No, no, no. I'm disappointed in you, Gal. Fills in the jigsaw indeed! From now on you just do the cables.

*(DVORNICHEK arrives with a tray on which there are a cognac and a revolting looking cocktail.)*

DVORNICHEK. Here we are, gentlemen! One cognac and a Mad Dog.

TURAI. At last. *(GAL takes the cognac. TURAI arrives at the tray too late.)* What is this muck?

DVORNICHEK. That's the surprise.

TURAI. I don't like surprises, especially when one is expecting cognac. How would *you* like it?

DVORNICHEK. Thank you, sir, most considerate - your health! But first - if I may be so bold - a toast! A toast to three passengers who have honoured the steamship *Italian Castle* by their embarkation at Cherbourg tonight bound for New York. To Sandor Turai and Alex Gal, world-famous playwrights and men of the theatre, friends and collaborators over twenty years and count-less comedies, dramas, light operettas, revues, sketches, lyrics and libretti, on five continents and in as many languages, joint authors, as ever, of the new comedy with music, *The Cruise of the Dodo! And* to their discovery, friend, protege, the young maestro, plucked from obscurity to imminent fame, their new composer, Adam Adam! - Coupled with their lovely leading lady in the room above* - the darling of the gods, Natasha Navrátilova, or

---

*Or 'next door', depending on the staging.

as she is known among the readers of the society pages ... Natasha Navratilóva! - Oh, and her leading man in D4, the matinée idol, Ivor Fish! Both of whom are now at dinner having boarded at Southampton earlier this afternoon! I raise my glass to your success in New York and I'm only sorry you're not taking the romantic lead yourself, Mr. Adam; I saw you last year at the Chapeau Rouge in *One, Two, Button My Cabbage* and you'd be better than Ivor Fish any jour of the semaine but let that pass, on behalf of the management I bid you welcome within the four walls of the *SS Italian Castle,* and may I say how thrilled I am personally that you have booked the Pisa Room for shipboard rehearsals! *(DVORNICHEK drains his glass.)*

TURAI. This is outrageous.

GAL. Thank you ... er ...

DVORNICHEK. Dvornichek.

GAL. Do you mind if I call you Murphy?

DVORNICHEK. Not at all, sir. Will there be anything else, sir?

GAL. Well, we're also having a little trouble with the ending.

DVORNICHEK. I know what you mean.

GAL. You do?

DVORNICHEK. Miss Navratilova was kind enough to let me read your play.

TURAI. Look, what does one have to do to get a drink round here?

GAL. Murphy, another cognac.

DVORNICHEK. Yes, sir.

GAL. And a little something to eat.

*(ADAM is trying to speak to DVORNICHEK.)*

DVORNICHEK. No problem ... *(to ADAM)* Dvornichek.

GAL. *(to TUARI)* That man could do a lot for *The Merchant of Venice.* He's got everything in except why Natasha isn't expecting us until the morning. *(DVORNICHEK is in the process of misunderstanding why ADAM is having difficulty addressing him.)*

DVORNICHEK. Dvornichek ... *(ADAM tries again.)* Murphy.

ADAM. *(Finally succeeding.)* I *know* I would but unfortunately, shortly after appearing in that revue at the Chapeau Rouge, I was struck by this curious disability which has made it impossible for me to continue my career as a performer.

DVORNICHEK. *(sympathetically)* Why, what's the problem?

TURAI. *(to DVORNICHEK)* Are you still here?!

DVORNICHEK. *(turning away from ADAM)* Yes, sir—

ADAM. *(just too late)* Timing.

DVORNICHEK. *(continuing)* Just off, sorry - you gentlemen caught me on the hop arriving by private launch in the middle of dinner. Miss Navratilova told me you were in Deauville working on the ending and would be joining the ship with the Cherbourg passengers in the morning after breakfast.

GAL. Yes, well—

DVORNICHEK. Don't tell me - you got tired of work, tired of Deauville, and Mr. Adam couldn't wait another night to be reunited with his lady-love.

GAL. *(gratefully)* Murphy - have a cognac.

DVORNICHEK. Thank you, sir! I'll be back in no time.

*(DVORNICHEK leaves.)*

TURAI. *(exasperated)* Are you paying that man?

GAL. *(to ADAM)* You know, Murphy's quite right. It's tragic that you can't play the role of Justine Deverell. Especially as we've got Ivor Fish. Ivor's very popular with the public, of course, a couple of hours of Ivor's company every eighteen months being just about right, but they don't knowingly get on boats with him. *(ADAM has been gearing up to speak.)*

ADAM. *(finally)* I could play it all right if only this ridiculous hesitation were the same each time.

TURAI. How do you mean?

ADAM. All I'd have to do is anticipate my lines.

GAL. That's a good idea. I see what you mean.

ADAM. Then I'd start speaking just as it's my turn.

GAL. Of course you would! Do you see what he's getting at, Turai?

ADAM. Unfortunately I can't time it.

GAL. But you're timing it perfectly!

ADAM. It's a matter of luck if I come in at the right moment.

GAL. Luck? What luck? You've solved it.

ADAM. It could go wrong at any moment because sometimes my voice comes out in a couple of seconds, sometimes I seem to be hesitating for minutes on end, and I never know which it's going to be.

GAL. *(ignoring him)* I'll cable New York. 'Fish overboard, a star is born.'

TURAI. Well, what is it normally, would you say?

GAL. We'll need costume fittings. What's your hat size?

ADAM. It varies according to my state of mind.

GAL. That's remarkable. What is it at the moment?

TURAI. *(to GAL)* Be quiet. *(to ADAM)* Perhaps the other actors could fill in until you're ready to speak, though it would be an enormous problem if the hesitation is too long.

GAL. What about your feet?

ADAM. Enormous.

GAL. Enormous feet.

TURAI. He's not talking to you! *(to ADAM)* What's the longest it's ever been?

ADAM. The longest was two days, that night at the Chapeau Rouge when it all began.

TURAI. Two days? The audience would have gone home.

ADAM. *(pause)* They did. *(pause)* I looked up in the middle of my first song and there at a table in the front row was my mother.

TURAI. And you fell silent for two days?

ADAM. I hadn't realized she'd got out of gaol. She'd been arrested in front of the Mona Lisa, which is where she'd spent a surprising part of her time since becoming convinced that she was the reincarnation of that lady, and I could tell by the enigmatic way she was smiling at me she hadn't changed a bit. I found I couldn't speak.

GAL. It had happened before?

ADAM. From childhood, every time she got out of gaol.

GAL. But why did they keep putting her in gaol?

ADAM. Assault, battery, attempted incestuous rape of a minor, and committing a nuisance in a public place, namely in front of the Mona Lisa.

GAL. Remarkable woman.

ADAM. Terrifying.

TURAI. Well you've given her the slip now.

ADAM. I hope so. But it's just as well we've got Ivor Fish, and I don't mind a bit who plays Natasha's lover so long as I'm her lover because Natasha is my muse and without her love I would fall silent truly and forever.

GAL. How the papers would have loved it. Adam Adam and Natasha Navratilova, the love birds on stage together every night, and it would have given the ending a wonderful quality, too, if we had an ending.

TURAI. We have four and a half days. We wrote *Lottie From Brest-Litovsk* in four and half days.

GAL. It also ran four and a half days. It was the first play ever to close after a matinee.

TURAI. That's because we didn't have Adam's music.

GAL. That's true. *(ADAM tries to speak.)* Don't say anything unless you have an ending.

ADAM. Or Natasha either.

TURAI. What?

ADAM. *(pause)* You didn't have my music or Natasha either.

GAL. Also true.

TURAI. And, don't forget, even if Deauville let us down with the ending, we have brought her a new song for the second act.

GAL. All true. With Adam's music and Natasha and the new song and a new ending and an Irish policeman, we shall have a wonderful success in New York if we do a little work on the middle ... even if we *are* stuck with Ivor.

TURAI. *(hopefully)* Ivor and Natasha have been very good together in the past, that play where Ivor had the motorbike ...

GAL. Yes, they had a wonderful eighteen months in *Pauline Rides Pillion,* and a *slightly* disappointing three weeks in *Romeo and Juliet.* God that was a mistake, people do the silliest things when they're in the middle of an...

TURAI. *(hurriedly)* I've got a wonderful idea! Let's welcome her back from dinner with the new song! Adam, go and get the score from your cabin, and a piano or something of the sort—

GAL. Yes, yes, and if she comes back we'll keep quiet as mice till you return and then we'll serenade her together with the new number. What do you think? *(ADAM tries to speak.)* Just nod. *(ADAM nods and leaves.)* I'm sorry. It slipped out.

TURAI. You know ... we should have sent her a telegram: "Arriving tonight".

GAL. Adam wanted to surprise her.

TURAI. He may succeed.

GAL. Oh, come now, all that was years ago. She was just a young girl flattered by an older man's attentions. Ivor was the bigger name then, and naturally one thing led to another, but everything's different now - she's a star and he's a middle-aged clod with a wife and four children and anyway she's in love with Adam - no, it's out of the question. *(He reflects.)* We should have sent a telegram.

TURAI. *(nodding gravely)* Never surprise a woman. They love surprises so long as they've been warned.

GAL. Look, I'm sure this isn't necessary but why don't I keep Adam busy until Natahsa is safely back in her room? Then let us know the good news and we'll all surprise her. We must have a happy composer to compose and a happy actress to sing and then we'll have a happy ending when we have an ending.

*(DVORNICKEK enters with a cognac and boiled potato on a tray.)*

DVORNICHEK. Here we are, sir, one cognac and a little something.

GAL. What's this?

DVORNICHEK. A boiled potato, sir.

GAL. *(taking it and leaving)* Thank you, Murphy.

TURAI. What kept you?

DVORNICHEK. You wouldn't beieve it. I went up the wrong staircase and found myself on the roof.

TURAI. *(irritated)* The top deck.

DVORNICHEK. And then I nearly fell down the trap door—

TURAI. *(exasperated)* Down the hatch, Murphy!

DVORNICHEK. Down the hatch, sir! *(He knocks back the brandy in one.)* — and tripped over a rope strung between bollocks.

TURAI. Look, would you please try to learn the proper names of things—

DVORNICHEK. Yes, sir. Will there be anything else, sir?

TURAI. *(faintly)* Perhaps a cognac.

DVORNICHEK. No problem, sir. *(solicitously and innocently)*

Is everything all right, sir?

TURAI. No. Everything —

*(At that moment he hears NATASHA'S VOICE singing from within her cabin.)*

TURAI. Yes! Yes, everything is fine, Murphy. Go and fetch - no, I'll go and fetch them. Get a bottle of champagne. Perrier. Jouet '21.

DVORNICHEK. Yes, sir.

TURAI. And four glasses.

DVORNICHEK. No problem. *(TURAI hurriedly follows DVORNICHEK out through the cabin. NATASHA'S VOICE still continues singing and she emerges on to her verandah, singing to herself.)*

NATASHA. *(sings)*
THIS COULD BE THE TIME.
NEVER BEEN SO FANCY FREE
TILL I KISSED YOU
AND YOU KISSED ME.
ISN'T IT SUBLIME?
THIS COULD BE THE TIME.
WHEN I SAW YOU
MY KNEES WENT WEAK
MY THROAT WENT DRY.
I COULD HARDLY SPEAK.

*(IVOR FISH in evening dress and holding a bottle of champagne and two glasses appears in the doorway and joins her on deck.)*

IVOR. Do you have to sing that song?

NATASHA. *(sings)*

ISN'T IT HEAVENLY?

I'm singing it because I like singing it, and because he wrote it for me to sing ... *(sings)*

TURTLE DOVES SANG TWO FOR TEA

YES, IT'S TRUE, WHEN I KISSED YOU

WEDDING BELLS RANG TEA FOR TWO

... and if it bothers you, you have your own cabin. *(sings)*

LA LA LA LA LA LA

In fact I don't know why you're not in it. I never invited you into mine.

IVOR. Natasha, Natasha, how can you forget?!

NATASHA. I haven't forgotten - you barged in and started opening my champagne.

IVOR. I *sent* you the champagne.

NATASHA. That's why it's mine.

IVOR. How can you speak to me like that? I was the love of your life!

NATASHA. That was another life. Now please go to bed, Ivor - it's very thoughtless of you to risk compromising me like this.

IVOR. I? I compromise you? I who discovered you? Is this the thanks I get? I who picked you for my pillion!

NATASHA. *(primly)* I've already thanked you for that.

IVOR. I who climbed up to your balcony!

NATASHA. *(coldly)* Only for three weeks.

IVOR. And what about this afternoon in that very cabin?

NATASHA. It's very bad form to dig up the past like this.

IVOR. Natasha!

NATASHA. I weakened for a moment when you said you'd kill yourself.

IVOR. You weakened for twenty-five minutes.

NATASHA. You said you'd exterminate your entire family. If you had any soul you would have understood that this afternoon was my farewell to that part of my life. I'm going to be a different woman from now on. My Adam will be here in the morning. He calls me his madonna. So there'll be no more of *that*.

IVOR. You don't love me?

NATASHA. No.

IVOR. I'll kill myself.

NATASHA. Now, now.

IVOR. I'll kill my wife and children and then myself.

NATASHA. It's no good, I'm not in the mood. Anyway, your wife is much more likely to kill *you* if she finds out what you're up to. You remember your wife? Piranha?

IVOR. Paloma. But she'd still kill me. *(heroically)* I'm willing to take the risk - do you want a man or a boy?

NATASHA. A boy.

IVOR. I'll kill him!

NATASHA. That would not be very sensible. If I know Gal and Turai those three will show up in the morning with half the second act still to come.

IVOR. *(unheroically)* Oh, how can you treat me like this when I love you so dreadfully.

NATASHA. Now don't be such a baby. I can't bear you to cry. Come on, you must go to bed.

IVOR. All right, I'll go. Only let me wait till you're

ready for bed so I can kiss you goodnight and then I swear I'll leave you.

NATASHA. All right. But you wait out here while I change, and no peeking.

IVOR. Oh, thank you, thank you, every moment is precious.

NATASHA. I'll only be a minute. *(NATASHA disappears inside continuing to sing to herself. IVOR stands looking moodily at the sea.)*

*(Below, TURAI, GAL and ADAM creep back into view and on to their deck. GAL carries sheet music and is eating a chicken leg. ADAM is carrying a banjo. TURAI takes charge in mime, getting the group into serenading position. Irritably he dispossesses GAL of his snack. He examines the manuscript score closely. When he is satisfied and everything is ready, he takes up the stance of a conductor. Above, NATASHA reappears having changed into a very beautiful but high-collared négligé. She pauses in the doorway as TURAI'S hand is about to descend.)*

NATASHA. There! I'm ready!

IVOR. My darling! *(The THREE TROUBADOURS freeze.)*

NATASHA. Now you may kiss me.

IVOR. My angel! *(The TROUBADOURS turn.)*

NATASHA. Now, you promised not to get carried away.

IVOR. I can't help it.

NATASHA. You're not going to begin again!

IVOR. Yes, again! *(The TROUBADOURS recoil in silent confusion.)* And again! And again!

TURAI. *(urbanely to ADAM)* This doesn't necessarily mean—

IVOR. I love you, I adore you, I worship you!

GAL. *(thoughtfully)* He's always been a tremendous fan of hers.

IVOR. I worship you as the moth worships the candle flame! *(TURAI gives a professional wince.)* I love you as the Eiffel Tower loves the little fleecy cloud that dances around it in the summer breeze. *(ADAM sits down.)*

NATASHA. You'll soon forget me!

IVOR. No, no, I'm mad about you. But you've plucked out my heart like the olive out of a dry Martini and dashed me from your lips! *(Despite everything, GAL and TURAI turn to each other in wonder.)*

NATASHA. Don't spoil everything we've had together. *(ADAM breaks a banjo string.)* Give me your hands - I will remember your hands, such clever, wicked hands, too, when I think of what they have done. *(ADAM breaks two more banjo strings.)* Please be a good boy - remember this afternoon. *(ADAM stands up.)* Here, let me kiss you.

IVOR. That's not a kiss. That's a tip!

NATASHA. Keep your voice down.

IVOR. I don't care. Let the whole world know that I mean nothing to you. I'm a dashed Martini!

TURAI. *(quietly to ADAM)* Come on—

NATASHA. That's not true - you will always be the first. I was a girl and you made me a woman. If I had *ten* husbands no one can take your place. *(ADAM takes the score from TURAI and rips it once across, and throws it down.)* But I'm engaged to be married so please be kind and leave me now. *(ADAM makes to leave but is given further pause by the next lines.)*

IVOR. All right, I will. Only let me see you as I want to

remember you. Lift your hair. Let me move your collar just a little.

NATASHA. Oh, you're impossible. What are you doing?

IVOR. One last look, one touch, I beg you! Oh, that pink rounded perfection! Let me put my lips to its rosy smoothness.

GAL. Her shoulder.

IVOR. And the other one!

GAL. Her other shoulder.

IVOR. How beautifully they hang there!

GAL. We should have sent a telegram.

NATASHA. Now stop it—

ADAM. I will throw myself overboard. *(ADAM leaves.)*

TURAI. *(to GAL)* Go with him. *(GAL leaves.)*

IVOR. Oh, forgive me.

NATASHA. I'll forgive you, you donkey, if only you'd go.

IVOR. I'm going now. Goodbye, Natasha, goodbye forever.

NATASHA. See you after breakfast. I'm going to be up early to meet Adam. And those two old rogues. *(TURAI looks pained.)* I do hope they've looked after my poor boy. *(TURAI looks even more pained.)*

IVOR. One more kiss! *(TURAI almost loses patience.)*

NATASHA. Good night, Ivor. There ... good night ...

IVOR. Good night. *(IVOR leaves.)*

NATASHA. *(sings)*

THIS COULD BE HEAVENLY
THIS COULD BE THE ONE.

*(NATASHA returns to her cabin.)*

Turai. At last. *(TURAI collapses into a chair or against the rail. NATASHA sings quietly for a few moments and then the soft light inside is extinguished. TURAI picks up the torn score.)*

*(GAL returns, eating.)*

Gal. All quiet? *(TURAI nods.)* Interesting silence? *(TURAI shakes his head.)*

Turai. He's gone. *(bitterly)* Eiffel Tower ... How's Adam?

Gal. He's fine. The banjo isn't so well.

Turai. Did he say anything?

Gal. He was trying.

Turai. Nodding his head, or shaking it?

Gal. Banging it against the wall.

Turai. Will you explain to me about you and food?

Gal. No.

Turai. I only eat once a day.

Gal. That's going to be a very convenient habit from now on.

Turai. It's the poor boy I'm worried about.

Gal. You don't have to worry about him - young people can always get their hands on a sandwich.

Turai. Look - we're being much too pessimistic. Natasha is a trouper and Adam will realize that his music means more to him than any woman.

Gal. Meanwhile he's torn up the rest of the score.

Turai. A gesture. Whish! - once across and tomorrow the glue. No?

Gal. It looks like a honeymoon suite in there. Without of course, the bride. *(venomously)* Fleecy little cloud ... she shouldn't be let out without a general alert. And as for that damned Martini ...

TURAI. Dashed.

GAL. *Dashed* Martini. Well, he certainly solved the problem of the ending: we won't be needing one.

TURAI. *(thoughtfully)* Yes ... yes ...

GAL. I'll cable New York. "Disembarked. Don't worry."

TURAI. Wait! I've got the strangest feeling ... that everything is going to be all right.

GAL. I think you need to eat something.

TURAI. Sssh! ... *(He freezes with intense concentration.)* We will have our premiére!

GAL. With Adam's music?

TURAI. With Adam's music, with Natasha, with an Irish policeman if you like! I feel it. I see light ... a vision ... I can't quite make it out but the edges are incandescent with promise! I see success - happiness - a wedding...

GAL. Low blood sugar.

TURAI. *(excitedly)* Stay with the boy! All night! Don't leave his side. Give him a sleeping pill.

GAL. I haven't got one.

TURAI. Don't be obtuse! Make him drunk! I want him asleep for eight hours at least. Tomorrow is going to be a day to test our mettle!

GAL. *(getting up)* Whatever you say. Make him drunk.

*(He goes towards the door and meets DVORNICHEK coming in with the champagne and the four glasses.)*

DVORNICHEK. Here we are, sir! Champagne!

TURAI. Excellent!

GAL. Perfect! *(GAL takes the champagne and two of the glasses and departs. Leaving.)* Good night, Turai!

TURAI. He took the champagne.

DVORNICHEK. Sorry I was so long. I've been all over. You wouldn't believe the cellar in this place - the *noise* -the *filth*—

TURAI. *(angrily)* That's the engine room!

DVORNICHEK. *(agreeing)* You don't have to tell me!

TURAI. Well, what were you doing there?

DVORNICHEK. A misunderstanding. American couple in E5, asked for two screwdrivers. First off, I can't find the doorman. So I get on the house phone for what I thought was the *bell* captain. 'Are you the captain?' I say. 'I am,' he says. 'Would you know where to put your hands on a couple of screwdrivers?' I say. Then the conversation deteriorates.

TURAI. Look, I've been trying to get a drink since I came on board.

DVORNICHEK. May I fetch you something, sir?

TURAI. Perhaps a cognac.

DVORNICHEK. Very good, sir.

TURAI. By the way...

DVORNICHEK. Yes, sir?

TURAI. Bring the bottle.

DVORNICHEK. No problem. *(DVORNICHEK leaves. TURAI whips out a gold pencil and starts scribbling in a notebook. He paces up and down in deep thought, occasionally making a note. DVORNICHEK returns with a bottle of brandy and a glass on his tray.* Shall I pour you one, sir?

TURAI. *(impatiently)* Yes, yes. Be quiet. *(He continues*

*making notes while DVORNICHEK opens the bottle and pours a glass of brandy. This empties the bottle. TURAI is suddenly satisfied. He relaxes. He accepts the glass from DVORNICHEK, sniffs it and holds it up to the light. As he is about to drink—)*

DVORNICHEK. Will you be requiring early morning tea, sir?

TURAI. Yes.

DVORNICHEK. What time?

TURAI. What time is it now?

DVORNICHEK. Coming up to one o'clock.

TURAI. I'll have it at half-past one, three o'clock, four-thirty and six.

DVORNICHEK. With milk or lemon?

TURAI. With cognac. Breakfast at seven.

DVORNICHEK. Yes, sir. *(TURAI raises his glass again, but—)*

DVORNICHEK. Tea or coffee?

TURAI. Black coffee. Half a grapefruit. Perhaps a little ham ... *(DVORNICHEK takes out a notebook and attempts to write down the order.)* Sausage, scrambled eggs, kidneys, a potato or two ... some cold cuts - chicken, beef, tongue, salami - oh, some kind of smoked fish, I'm not fussy - cheese, white rolls, brown toast, a couple of croissants ... *(DVORNICHEK is still trying to organize himself to write down the first item. TURAI impatiently puts down his glass and snatches DVORNICHEK'S notebook and continues, scribbling in the notebook.)* Butter, strawberry jam, honey, pancakes and some stewed fruit. *(TURAI hands back the notebook. DVORNICHEK picks up the silver salver on which TURAI has replaced his untouched drink.)*

DVORNICHEK. Cream?

TURAI. *(sharply)* No. *(then relenting)* Well, a little. I only
eat once a day. Do you know what is the most important
thing in life?

DVORNICHEK. Yes, sir.

TURAI. Good health.

DVORNICHEK. Thank you, sir. Good health! *(He drains
TURAI's glass.)* Tea in half an hour. I'll make it myself.

TURAI. Thank you, er...

DVORNICHEK. Murphy.

TURAI. Thank you, Murphy.

DVORNICHEK. Thank you, sir. *(DVORNICHEK leaves.
Transition into interior of TURAI's cabin. A silver tea service, cup
and saucer, without any tray, are on the writing desk. TURAI's
impressive breakfast has arrived on a trolley and DVORNICHEK
is laying out a breakfast table. TURAI can be heard singing cheerfully offstage. TURAI enters looking rejuvenated, showered,
shaved, well scrubbed and in elegant yachting clothes. DVOR-
NICHEK laying out the breakfast, greets him cheerfully.)*

DVORNICHEK. Ahoy there! Seven bells and all's well!
the sun's over the yardarm and there's a force three east-
sou'-easterly with good visibility. Where do you want
the vittles?

TURAI. Who are you?

DVORNICHEK. Murphy, sir.

TURAI. I see you've picked up the lingo.

DVORNICHEK. Speak it like a native, sir. Had to put in a
bit of spurt. They're getting suspicious about me being
on the *Mauretania.*

TURAI. Really? What happened?

DVORNICHEK. It's that captain again. Half-past five he
phones down for a cup of Ovaltine and a chocolate bis-

cuit. 'Where are you?' I say. 'On the bloody bridge, where do you think I am?' he says. 'Jump to it.' So I jump to it, and I'm looking both ways along the veranda but none of the bridges are out and by the time I find him pacing up and down the front balcony he's absolutely demented, threatened to have me ironed in the clappers. How was your night?

TURAI. Quite successful, thank you. *(He is lifting various silver domes on the table.)* I can't see the smoked fish.

DVORNICHEK. Starboard of the coffee pot.

TURAI. Oh, yes. *(TURAI sits down and DVORNICHEK pours coffee. From now on he starts tucking into his breakfast. DVORNICHEK goes to clear up the teapot, etc.)*

DVORNICHEK. What happened to the tray?

TURAI. Never mind that. Would you lift up that telephone and speak to Miss Navratilova and then Mr. Fish. Present my compliments, apologize for the hour and ask them to join me.

DVORNICHEK. Aye, aye, sir. *(He lifts the phone. Into phone, conversationally:)* Ahoy there. Please connect me with Miss Navratilova.

TURAI. And then see that we are not disturbed.

DVORNICHEK. Not even by Mr. Gal and Mr. Adam?

TURAI. Especially not by them.

DVORNICHEK. Aye aye sir. *(into phone)* Yes, miss. It's Dvornichek. Yes, miss, I'm speaking from Mr. Turai's cabin. Yes, he's here and he presents his comp - *(She has hung up. He replaces the telephone.)* I think she's coming. *(He lifts the telephone again. Into phone:)* Ahoy again. Connect me with Mr. Fish in D4 please.

TURAI. You don't have to keep saying ahoy.

Dvornichek. Aye, aye, sir. *(into phone)* Yes, he's rather hard to wake ... no problem, I'll go and bang on his door. Bon voyage. *(He puts the phone down.)* Will that be all, sir?

Turai. No. *(He hands DVORNICHEK a slip of paper.)* I want you to send this telegram for me. It's to go to Mr. Adam Adam, c/o the SS *Italian Castle* en route to New York.

Dvornichek. Fast rate or overnight?

Turai. Fast rate. In fact he'll be joining me in here within half an hour: I want you to deliver it as soon as I ring that bell.

Dvornichek. No problem.

Turai. Are you sure?

Dvornichek. Am I sure what?

Turai. Nothing. The telegraph office, you'll recall, is on the starboard side.

Dvornichek. Right.

Turai. Up by the chimneys.

Dvornichek. We don't call them the chimneys, sir. We call them the smokesticks.

Turai. That will do.

Dvornichek. Yes, sir.

*(DVORNICHEK goes to the door and meets NATASHA coming in.)*

Dvornichek. Good morning!

Natasha. Hello, Dvornie. *(She sees TURAI. DVOR-NICHEK leaves, closing the door.)* Sandor! Darling! How wonderful! Are you all here? Alex? And my Adam?

TURAI. All aboard.

NATASHA. You early birds! It must have been dawn.

TURAI. No, it was while you were having dinner.

NATASHA. What? - you've been there all night? For God's sake, why didn't you tell me? I would have ordered champagne! You idiot! I was up till midnight and my cabin is *literally* up *above*. You'd only have had to raise your voi-oi-oi-oi - No.

TURAI. Yes.

NATASHA. Oh no.

TURAI. Oh yes.

NATASHA. But only you.

TURAI. No.

NATASHA. You and Alex?

TURAI. No.

NATASHA. *(under sentence of death)* Adam?

TURAI. Every word. *(He is placidly eating breakfast. She lunges at the table and grabs a knife.) (calmly)* That won't do any good.

NATASHA. You don't know me, Sandor! I have Romany blood in my veins!

TURAI. I mean, it's a fish knife. *(She throws the knife down and collapses into a chair sobbing.)*

NATASHA. Where's Adam?

TURAI. Asleep, I trust. I made Gal stay with him.

NATASHA. He called me his madonna. Oh, Sandor, you're the only one who knows how I love him

TURAI. No, as I say, it was all three of us.

NATASHA. Don't be cruel! I'm the victim of my own generosity. Ivor is so pathetic - he keeps bursting into tears telling me to remember the old days on the pillion.

*(viciously)* It was all that shaking up and down on the pillion which got me into this! I swear to you it's over - last night was the last flicker of the candle flame.

*(There is an angry KNOCKING on the door.)*

TURAI. Here comes the moth.

*(The door opens and IVOR comes in wearing pyjamas and dressing-gown.)*

TURAI. Good morning, Ivor.

IVOR. What the devil is going on - I was asleep. *(Then he sees NATASHA.)* Oh - good morning, my dear.

TURAI. I'm sorry to wake you.

IVOR. Actually I didn't close my eyes till dawn ... tossing, turning, pacing the floor—

NATASHA. Oh, shut up.

IVOR. Is everything all right?

NATASHA. No.

TURAI. Sit down. Our little show is in trouble.

IVOR. You haven't done the ending. Honestly, Turai, one likes to give you writer johnnies a bit of leeway but—

TURAI. *(thunders)* Silence! *(He points witheringly at IVOR.)* Eiffel Tower! Dashed Martini!

IVOR. When did you get here?

TURAI. Last night while you were having dinner, we got aboard, unpacked a few things and sat on the sundeck in the moonlight to wait for you. *(IVOR goes out and inspects the geography of the adjacent sundecks. He comes back.*

IVOR. You and Gal. *(NATASHA starts to weep again.)*

IVOR. And Adam. I'm a dead man if this gets out.

TURAI. Yes, how *is* Mrs. Fish?

IVOR. *(in panic)* He wouldn't tell her? What did he say?

TURAI. He said he was going to cut your part to ribbons and post it to her.

IVOR. *(aghast but also surprised)* He said that?

TURAI. He was trying to.

.NATASHA. Poor love, poor handicapped little love! See what you've done, you selfish monster - ruined his life, and mine! Oh, to die - to die!

IVOR. *(heroically)* Together! Like Romeo and Juliet! *(He snatches up a piece of cutlery.)*

TURAI. That's a spoon.

NATASHA. *(to TURAI:)* How much did he hear? When I think of those silly things one says ... Was it from the moment we got back until Ivor left?

TURAI. Not quite. Roughly from Eiffel Tower to pink rounded perfection.

NATASHA. *(cries out)* He knows about that one?

TURAI. And the other one. The question is, how can we repair the harm. I mean to the boy. My only thought is for the boy.

NATASHA. So young, so brilliant ... so damaged!

IVOR. If only it had been his *ears.*

NATASHA. Shut up, you brute!

TURAI. Yes, do be quiet, Ivor. I'm trying to get you both out of this mess.

NATASHA. There's no way.

TURAI. There is. I am about to pull the rabbit out of the hat.

NATASHA. You have a rabbit?

TURAI. I have.

NATASHA. Sandor, I'll be your slave for life, I'll put myself under contract - I'll - *(caution intercedes)* What is it?

TURAI. What you were doing in your cabin last night was learning your parts? Do you understand?

NATASHA. Yes! No.

TURAI. Your conversation, which we partly overheard, was not a conversation, it was a rehearsal.

NATASHA. *(awestruck)* That's *brilliant!* *(and immediately irritated)* That's *stupid* - where on earth are we ever going to find a play with lines like that in it?

TURAI. *(indicating the desk)* Over there. *(NATASHA goes to the desk.)*

NATASHA. Here?

TURAI. You hold it in your hands.

NATASHA. *(understanding)* Of course ... ! Sandor...

IVOR. You found one?

NATASHA. Be quiet, Ivor. Sandor, how do you do it?

TURAI. Either one is a playwright or one is not.

IVOR. You wrote it?

TURAI. I did. And never was anything written with truer purpose. Never! We each fight life's battle with the weapons God gave us. Mine is theatre. Alas. But today I feel like a Greek athlete at the Battle of Marathon. Yes, he thinks, yes, for once there seems to be something *to* this javeline business. *(NATASHA is looking through TURAI's manuscript pages.)*

NATASHA. 'I love you as the Eiffel Tower loves the little fleecy cloud that dances—' *(IVOR snatches the page from her.*

*She reads from the next page.)*

NATASHA. 'You have plucked out my heart like the olive out of a dry Martini—'

TURAI. It reads better than it plays. But you've played it once so you can play it again.

NATASHA. What do you mean? Do we have to *do* it?

TURAI. Of course. Who will believe you otherwise? Rehearsal this afternoon, two o'clock sharp in the Pisa Room. Adam will be there so make sure you've learned it.

IVOR. I can't learn all this in a morning.

TURAI. Why not? You knew it well enough last night.

NATASHA. I never said, 'No one can take your place.'

TURAI. Yes, you did.

NATASHA. Well, I didn't mean it.

IVOR. You didn't?

NATASHA. Of course I didn't. A *budgerigar* could take your place!

IVOR. You bitch!

NATASHA. I hate you!

TURAI. It's too late now - last night was the time for that. Off you go. There's a copy for each of you.

IVOR. Excue me - why are we rehearsing this new piece when we're supposed to be in the middle of rehearsals for *The Cruise of the Dodo?*

NATASHA. *(to IVOR:)* Oh. don't be so — *(to TURAI:)* Why *are* we rehearsing this new piece?

TURAI. It's not a new piece it's the new ending.

NATASHA. That's brilliant. That's stupid! We can't go

on stage and say these stupid things! We'd be a laughing
stock! 'I worship you as the moth worships the candle
flame'!

IVOR. *(hurt)* What's wrong with that?

NATASHA. *(to TURAI:)* And just to put your rabbit out
of its misery, may I ask why we're rehearsing in my cabin
at midnight?

TURAI. Quite simple. Gal and I were due to arrive in
the morning. It was your last chance to polish up your
surprise for us.

IVOR. What surprise?

TURAI. Your new ending.

IVOR. Mine?!

TURAI. Well, of course. Who's going to believe that I
wrote that bilge? And anyway, I couldn't have written it
because I would have recognized it. No, what happened
was that you two knew damned well that Gal and I would
get nowhere in Deauville so you thought you'd have a
crack at it yourself.

NATASHA. He can't write.

IVOR. I can't write.

TURAI. *(sadly)* I know. He has a certain gift for
construction.

IVOR. Oh, do I?

TURAI. He tells the story, but he doesn't understand
character. *(squeezing IVOR'S shoulder)* Touched, all the
same, I'll let you down gently, count on me. The new
scene takes off from the line, 'Mother is coming up for
sale this afternoon.'

NATASHA and IVOR. 'Mother is coming up for sale
this afternoon.'

TURAI. We will rehearse the old ending and when we

all agree that it needs something, Ivor will say, 'Actually, Turai, while you were in Deauville I put pen to paper and Natasha and I have worked up a little scene which you may care to to have a look at', and I will say, 'My dear Ivor, I'm touched beyond measure, do let's see what you've been up to', and then off you go from 'Mother is coming up for sale', and Bob's your uncle, I don't see how anything can go wrong. Meanwhile you have a busy morning, so back to your cabins. *(IVOR sighs.)*

TURAI.  Don't sigh like that.

IVOR.  It was a sigh of relief. Paloma, you know.

TURAI.  Don't worry about her. She has other fish to fry. Now, don't forget, when next we meet you haven't seen me for a week.

IVOR.  Until two o'clock then. *(IVOR leaves.)*

NATASHA.  Sandor, you've done it. Did Gal help?

TURAI.  No. He knows nothing. I thought after twenty years of marriage I'd treat myself to a night out. Until two o'clock, and don't forgot you're my slave for life.

NATASHA.  *(kissing him)* The things one says when one's back is to the rail. *(NATASHA leaves. TURAI goes to the telephone and lifts the receiver.)*

TURAI.  *(into phone:)* Good morning. This is Sandor Turai. Would you please connect me with Mr. Gal? Oh really?

How kind of you to say so.

Well, it's just a gift, really.

Sometimes the words before the music, sometimes the music before the words.

I don't really have a favourite.

Actually, that was written by two other people.

It's perfectly all right.

Oh, have you?

Well, unfortunately I haven't got much time to read nowadays. Mr. Gal would love to read it. Why don't I ask him? Yes, why don't you, he is in Cabin B2 at the moment.

Thank you so much. *(pause)*

Gal, are you awake?

Don't be a pedant.

Well, I'm sorry.

Half-past seven or so. Is Adam awake?

What do you mean?

Well, where is he?

You incompetent! - I said get *him* drunk!

Well, you'd better go out and find him! I don't know - look in the water. Do I have to do everything for you? I already do the plot, the characterization, the better jokes and binding contracts - if anything's happened to the boy I'll get someone else to do the cables! —

*(There's a KNOCK at the door.)*

Come in. *(continuing)* Don't you practise your economy of empression on *me* you drunken - *(He sees that it is ADAM who has entered.)* My dear boy! Come in - *(into phone:)* Adam has just come in. *(to ADAM:)* Would you like some breakfast - coffee? *(into phone:)* So glad you had a good night's rest, dear chap, why don't you get up now and join us. The sun's over the yardarm and it's a beautiful day with a fresh north-south-easterly breeze with good visibility.

*(He sees that GAL has entered.)* Hello, Gal, come in—

*He does a double-take at the telephone in his hand and puts it down. GAL is wearing last night's clothing and looking worse for wear. ADAM is wearing what is clearly a disembarkation outfit - including hat and topcoat. He does not have his luggage with him but is carrying, perhaps, an attaché case, which GAL and TURAI affect not to notice. ADAM offers his hand to GAL in farewell. GAL shakes it casually.)*

GAL. Good morning, Adam.

ADAM. ... *(ADAM offers his hand to TURAI, who shakes it vigorously.)*

TURAI. *(cheerfully)* Good morning! You're looking wonderfully refreshed. Been for a walk? Not much of a town, is it?

ADAM. ...

GAL. Had breakfast? I hardly bother with it myself.

ADAM. ...

TURAI. Don't try to talk. Have some coffee.

ADAM. ...

TURAI. I know, I know. But we can ring for a cup. *(TURAI goes to a bell push and presses it long and firmly.)* I know what you're going to say. You've woken up a new man. You laugh at love like this - ha! - ha! You snap your fingers at it like *that (snap!)* - you are free of the tyrannies of the heart. Nothing else matters to you but to hear your music played. You are an artist. For you there are no more women, only Woman, the female spirit that remains constant while the Natashas and the Marias and the Zsa Zsas come and go, each seeming for a moment to embody the idea, each giving way to the next, illusory, inconstant, all too human, unequal to the artist's measure, unworthy of his lute.

GAL.  That gives you an idea of the sort of plays he'd be writing if he didn't have me to stop him. *(GAL has been picking at the ample leftovers of TURAI's breakfast.)*

TURAI.  Would you be good enough to order your own breakfast?

GAL.  It's as much as I can do to pick at something to keep my strength up.

ADAM.  *(finally)* Goodbye! *(pause)* I'm sorry.

TURAI.  Adam, I'm astonished. And yet, I understand. First love. The pain of it all. But take the advice of an older man.

GAL.  Try the kippers.

TURAI.  Wait!

GAL.  Wait till you've tried the kippers.

TURAI.  Wait! - Because while you wait, fate's caravan moves on. Do nothing! Say nothing! Wait!

GAL.  It's no good. I can't swallow. My throat is constricted.

TURAI.  Yes, I know. You want to kill yourself. Or her. Or Ivor. I understand, Especially in the case of Ivor. But stay your hand - for an hour - two hours - where the hell is that steward?

*(TURAI presses the bell yet more firmly.)*

ADAM.  My luggage is at the top of the gangway and when the boat sails in ten minutes it will sale without me for my muse is dead and as for me I will never write music again!

GAL. My dear boy, you're talking nonsense. I know about writer's block. What you need is a cooked breakfast.

TURAI. Adam, sit down and keep calm!

ADAM. How can you speak of breakfast when it's the end of everything and my music is a thousand scraps of paper floating away on the tide, I thought you were my friends—

GAL. We are, we really are - is there any cream?

TURAI. No!

GAL. No *cream?*

TURAI. No! - Let the boy be. Adam, I'm sorry. I have no right. You must do as you wish. Your life is your own. If you must go, then go you must, and God be with you. And, by the way, there is something I would like you to have, a negligible piece of the Turai family silver which I was going to give you on the occasion of your American debut - please, no argument - let it be a momento of happy days spent together in the vineyard of musical comedy. The fruit stayed on the vine but there will be other seasons, and ripeness is all. *(TURAI has detached himself to produce a flat parcel wrapped in tissue paper from which flutters a white envelope containing as it happens a white card. TURAI presents the parcel with great dignity. ADAM seems moved. ADAM takes off the envelope and removes the card and reads it silently. He is even more moved. He embraces TURAI and kisses him on both cheeks. ADAM places the card on the table and begins to unwrap the parcel. GAL picks up the card and reads from it.)*

GAL. 'Homard, maestro.' Is it a lobster?

TURAI. *(taking the card from GAL)* 'Homage, maestro ... all for one and one for all ... *(ADAM has now revealed a silver tray.)* I hope you like it - made of silver washed from the upper Danube, one of the last pieces - the family silver is sadly depleted and dispersed. You see it's engraved with the Turai motto, *Festina lente.* Every lent a festival. That's us Turais I'm afraid! - irrepressible! Gal, press the bell, we must drink Adam's health before he goes.

ADAM. Wait! I cannot leave you like this...

TURAI. *(relieved)* My dear boy...

ADAM. *(Changes his mind.)* But I must. Goodbye!

*(DVORNICHEK enters with a telegram envelope borne ceremoniously on a silver tray.)*

DVORNICHEK. Your telegram.

TURAI. Ah! Just in time.

DVORNICHEK. It's for Mr. Adam.

TURAI. So it is. Gal - a telegram for Adam. *(to DVOR-NICHEK:)* You call this fast rate?

DVORNICHEK. This boat was designed by a lunatic. When you're coming from the front starboard's on the left. *(ADAM is eveidently taken aback by the telegram. He looks at the envelope carefully. Meanwhile GAL is studying ADAM's tray.)*

GAL. 'Festina lente.'

DVORNICHEK. 'Make haste slowly.'

TURAI. Thank you, Murphy.

DVORNICHEK. No problem.

GAL. 'Festina lente ... C.L.' What's the C.L.?

TURAI. That's the date.

GAL. One hundred and fifty. That's early.

TURAI. I mean the weight.

DVORNICHEK. Castle Line.

TURAI. That will be all, Murphy. Champagne and four glasses.

DVORNICHEK. *(leaving)* Four? You're too kind. *(As DVORNICHEK closes the door behind him, ADAM, who has opened the telegram and read it and gone into a freeze, starts to have a minor convulsion.*

GAL. Adam, what is it?

TURAI. Not bad news, I hope? *(ADAM collapses into a chair, letting the telegram fall to the floor. GAL picks it up and reads it.)*

GAL. *(reads)* 'Arriving Cherbourg - disembark and embrace your ever devoted mother.'

TURAI. It seems your mother has tracked you down. *(ADAM stands, takes off coat.)* Changed your mind? *(to GAL:)* Telephone Natasha's cabin. Explain that we have arrived on board and ask her to join us. *(to ADAM:)* Sit down, Adam.

GAL. *(into phone:)* Good morning.

TURAI. Now listen.

GAL. *(into phone:)* This is Alex Gal. Would you connect me with—

TURAI. You can remain on one condition.

GAL. *(into phone:)* Oh really? How kind of you to say so.

TURAI. You must behave as though nothing has happened. Otherwise you might as well pack yourself off on the Paris train with your mother and leave us to start again with a new composer.

GAL. *(into phone:)* Mostly me. He works under my supervision.

TURAI. *(His attention caught.)* Just a moment.

GAL. *(into phone:)* Oh, have you? All about a telephone operator, eh? What a good idea.

TURAI. *(resuming)* Because we have four and a half days. We can manage a musical comedy, but we can't afford a melodrama.

GAL. *(into phone:)* Well, unfortunately I haven't got time to read, but why don't I ask Miss Navratilova...

TURAI. In short, your score and your presence are worse than useless without your absolute discretion.

GAL. *(into phone:)* Natasha? It's Alex! I'm with Turai ... yes and Adam of course. Come and - I think she's coming. *(He puts the phone down.)*

TURAI. So what is it going to be? On one side - courage, dignity, style and my respect. On the other side - mother. *(ADAM stands up. He screws up the telegram and then picks up the silver tray. He stands before TURAI trying to speak.)*

ADAM. *(finally)* With this piece of silver you have made me of your family. I am a Turai and I will obey you.

TURAI. *(joyfully)* I knew you could do it! It will be as though last night never happened. In fact last night we were on shore. We have arrived this morning with a precious gift, our new song for Natasha, and we shall present our gift when she enters and show her who can and who cannot be counted on when it comes to delivering the goods!

*(There is a KNOCK at the door. TURAI indicates that ADAM*

*should open it. ADAM does so and NATASHA steps into the cabin.
ADAM and NATASHA look at each other for a moment and then
kiss, a little warily despite the pretence which each has to maintain.
TURAI and GAL are poised to sing the song for NATASHA. The
THREE MEN start to do this, using cutlery to accompany themselves by setting up a percussion beat on the various pots and dishes
and silver domes on TURAI's breakfast table.*

*The song may be sung as a trio or distributed between the three
men. The lines 'up or down' and 'round and round' may be given to
ADAM solo, in which case ADAM'S hesitation makes a momen-
tary hiatus in the song.*

*After* "You have a volunteer" *the ship's HOOTER sounds and
NATASHA says: "You're here! And just in time!" [and she could
plausibly join in on the last two lines.])*

*Where do we go from here?*

WE JUST SAID HELLO AND HOW DO YOU DO,
AND BOTH OF US KNOW I'M LEAVING WITH
  YOU,
THE SIGNS ARE ALL TOO CLEAR
BUT WHERE DO WE GO FROM HERE?

WE'LL SAIL THROUGH THE NIGHT,
AND SLEEP THROUGH THE DAY,
WE'RE TRAVELLING LIGHT,
LET'S GO ALL THE WAY.
IT SOUNDS A NICE IDEA—
BUT WHERE DO WE GO FROM HERE?

THIS WAY, THAT WAY, UP OR DOWN
WE COULD GO BOTH WAYS.
FORWARD, BACKWARDS, ROUND AND ROUND,
WHAT DO I CARE
SO LONG AS WHEN WE GET TOGETHER
AND YOU'RE RESTLESS AGAIN
AND CLOSING YOUR GRIP
AND YOU NEED A FRIEND
TO HELP WITH THE ZIP,
YOU HAVE A VOLUNTEER
SO WHERE DO WE GO—
WHEN DO WE GO—
DARLING I'M SO READY TO GO—
SO WHY DON'T WE GO FROM HERE?

# ACT TWO

*A 'salon' aboard the Italian Castle ... this would be a moderately splendid public room available for private hire. There are entrances upstage Right and Left on a raised section, and the body of the room is approached down a short Central staircase, perhaps only a few steps. The space has been fairly cleared.*

*One table however, is preserved to accommodate a fairly elaborate buffet.*

*The salon contains a telephone.*

*There is also a baby grand piano. ADAM is at the piano. GAL is at the buffet.*

*We are in mid rehearsal. NATASHA and IVOR are singing a duet. They are not 'in costume'. After the first verse they go straight into the dialogue of the rehearsal.*

*TURAI, who is nominally in charge, divides his time between watching placidly from one side and reading a newspaper.*

*This Could Be The One*

NATASHA and IVOR.
THIS COULD BE THE ONE,

49

NEVER KNEW THE SKY SO BLUE
TILL YOU KISSED ME AND I KISSED YOU.
WHEN ALL'S SAID AND DONE,
THIS COULD BE THE ONE.

NATASHA. Justin, I've been looking everywhere for you.

IVOR. Have you?

NATASHA. Oh, Justin! I need your help. Actually it's mother.

IVOR. Have you thought of asking Reggie Robinsod?

NATASHA. Reggie Robinsod? Why do you say that?

IVOR. *(lapsing)* It's the way it's typed. *(pause)* Oh, right. *(resuming)* Have you thought of asking Reggie Robinsod?

NATASHA. It's Reggie who's the cause of the trouble. He has telegraphed the Italian police to arrest Mother as soon as the Dodo reaches Naples!

IVOR. I'm sorry to say this, Ilona, but your mother's arrest is long overdue. I don't know why she is still at large.

NATASHA. Justin!

IVOR. Your mother gives a chap pause, Ilona. As a matter of fact, your mother would give anybody pause, even two or three chaps working as a team. Pause, if we're going to be open about this, is what your mother would give Mussolini ... so don't worry your pretty little head about the Italian police, and tell your mother not to worry her pretty enormous one either.

NATASHA. Justin!

IVOR. It was the sight of your mother, Ilona which

made me hesitate to propose to you until fully three hours after I saw you standing here at this rail when I came aboard at Monte Carlo. I noticed her on deck when I was halfway up the gangplank. 'That's jolly nice!' I said to myself, taking her to be a small bandstand, and then I heard you say 'Good morning, Mother' and the words, 'Will you marry me whoever you are' froze upon my lips.

NATASHA. Justin! *(to TURAI:)* Look, is that all I get to say? He's walking all over my mother with his smart remarks and all I do is bleat 'Justin'.

TURAI. Well we can stop to criticize my work or we can get on to more important matters.

NATASHA. *(getting the point immediately)* Justin!

IVOR. I feel I can speak freely about your mother now, now that you have evidently broken off our secret engagement.

NATASHA. Justin! *(to TURAI:)* Good.

IVOR. I must have been blind! Last night when you kissed me on the stern *(lapsing)*... Do you think that might be misunderstood? I'll make it the poop, shall I? *(resuming)* Last night when you kissed me on the poop ... *(lapsing)* well, how about the sundeck?

GAL. In the moonlight.

IVOR. Last night when you kissed me on the sundeck in the moonlight—

GAL. Forget the sundeck.

IVOR. Last night when you kissed me in the moonlight it was Reggie Robinsod who was in your thoughts.

NATASHA. Justin!

GAL. Reggie.

NATASHA. Reggie! How could you think—?

IVOR. How could I not? Ilona, last night when you kissed me I gave you a pledge of my love, a single emerald ear-ring which had once been worn by the Empress Josephine and has been in my mother's family since the day the Little Corporal tossed it from his carriage window to my maternal ancestor Brigadier Jean-Francois Perigord de St Emilion who had escorted him into exile. That jewel was our secret, but it has betrayed you. Here it is.

NATASHA. Where did you find that?

IVOR. Where you left it - in Reggie's cabin!

NATASHA. Reggie!

GAL. Justin.

NATASHA. Justin!

IVOR. Yes. I looked in on him before breakfast to tell him I had booked the ping-pong table. He had already left. As I was closing the door something by his bed caught my eye. It was Empress Josephine's ear-ring. Say nothing, Ilona. There is nothing to be said. I know that Reggie Robinsod has money while I have nothing but the proud name of Deverell.

NATASHA. Not even that, Justin. Your name isn't Deverell and never has been.

IVOR. Ilona!

NATASHA. It is Tomkins!

IVOR. Ilona!

NATASHA. I wanted to give you the chance to tell me yourself. I would have forgiven you. Now it's too late.

IVOR. But how—?

NATASHA. I thought I knew you the moment I caught

sight of you coming up the gangplank. When I saw your forehand top-spin it came back to me - Bobby Tomkins who won the ping-pong tournament at the Hotel des Bains on the Venice Lido in '26. I confess I was a little in love with you even then.

IVOR. Well! So neither of us is quite what we seem, Ilona. Perhaps we belong together after all.

NATASHA. There's one more thing I haven't told you.

IVOR. What is that?

NATASHA. This! *(NATASHA sweeps back her lovely hair from one ear, dramatically.)*

IVOR. *(gasps)* Josephine's other ear-ring!

NATASHA. Ear-rings come in pairs, after all, Justin.

GAL. Bobby.

NATASHA. Bobby. Reggie Robinsod is the rightful owner of the emerald ear-rings. One of them disappeared years ago and ended up, God know how, in the innocent possession of my mother, unregarded and unrecognised until last night when Reggie noticed it among her trinkets. He called my mother a thief and left to telegraph the Naples police, taking the emerald back to his cabin, where you found it! As for this one which you gave me, it was stolen recently from his suite in the Grand Hotel in Monte Carlo - wasn't it, Tomkins?

IVOR. I cannot deny it.

NATASHA. *(passionately)* Oh, tell me it was just a moment of madness! You're not really a jewel thief.

IVOR. I am. I have always been. I was the village jewel thief and I went on from there - regional - national - international! I've been stealing ear-rings, necklaces, bracelets and the occasional tiara all my adult life.

NATASHA. But why?

IVOR. Who knows? Perhaps I was starved of affectation as a child. *(lapsing)* That's a typing error, is it? *(a hostile silence)* Oh I see. While we've stopped, how would some corporal get hold of the Empress Josephine's ear-rings? Does that seem odd to anybody? *(pause)* Right. *(resuming)* I didn't go to Reggie's cabin to ask about ping-pong - I waited until he left and then went to steal whatever I could find. I might as well be frank.

NATASHA. Frank!

GAL. Bobby!

NATASHA. Bobby! Oh what a fool you've been! You must have known something was up when you found the ear-ring in the cabin of the very man you stole it from!

IVOR. The name Reggie Robinsod meant nothing to me. The hotel room which I burgled belonged to the shipping magnate Sir Reginald Sackville-Stew.

NATASHA. You mean Reggie Robinsod is Sir Reginald Sackville-Stew of the Sackville-Stew Line, owner of the Dodo?

IVOR. *(lapsing)* They'll never follow this, you know. And we haven't even got to the complicated bit when it turns out that after the child was stolen in Harrods while the Sackville-Stew nanny was buying sensible shoes the first ear-ring was found in Ilona's potty.

NATASHA. What potty? The ear-ring was clutched in my little fist.

IVOR. It was in your potty.

NATASHA. It's obscene, my script says fist.

IVOR. All the others say potty.

NATASHA. *(leaving)* Right.

GAL. Fist.

NATASHA. *(returning)* Thank you.

IVOR. Well what are you going to do, Ilona?

NATASHA. I have no choice. My mother has been branded a common thief. I must clear her name and tell the Italian police everything I know, including, come to think of it, my suspicions concerning the several robberies at the Hotel des Bains in Venice the year Bobby Tomkins won the ping-pong singles under his real name.

IVOR. It wasn't actually. I've used many names.

NATASHA. Well, what is your name?

IVOR. Gerald something. They'll have it at Haileybury if you really want to know. I still have the cups for cross-country and boxing somewhere. The police were called but they never suspected me. In fact I've never been caught for anything. I was always too careful ... until I fell in love!

*(ADAM, at the piano, picks up the tune again.)*

NATASHA. I wish I knew what to do, Justin!

GAL. Gerald.

NATASHA. Gerald. *(IVOR and NATASHA go back into the song.)*

IVOR.

WHEN I SAW YOU
MY KNEES WENT WEAK
MY THROAT WENT DRY,

I COULD HARDLY SPEAK,
  Natasha.
ISN'T IT HEAVENLY.
  Both.
THIS COULD BE THE ONE!
GLORY BE, WHEN YOU KISSED ME
TURTLE DOVES SANG TWO FOR TEA,
  Ivor.
YES IT'S TRUE,
WHEN I KISSED YOU,
WEDDING BELLS RANG TEA FOR TWO.
  Natasha.
WANT TO JUMP THE GUN?
THIS COULD BE HEAVENLY
THIS COULD BE ...
  Turai. Now you kiss her! ...

*(They kiss demurely. Somewhere round here, DVORNICHEK enters with a cognac on a tray, heading for TURAI.)*

  Turai. You call that a kiss? Again! *(They kiss again, a little less demurely.)* No, no, as if you meant it!

*(IVOR and NATASHA kiss more convincingly, and ADAM bangs all the piano keys and leaps up ... just as DVORNICHEK is carrying the cognac past him. ADAM sweeps the cognac off the tray and downs it in one. DVORNICHEK, his attention distracted, innocently offers the empty tray to TURAI.)*

  Turai. Don't worry, Adam, I quite understand - it must be agony for you. *(to DVORNICHEK:)* Cognac.

DVORNICHEK. *(leaving)* No problem.

NATASHA. *(nervously)* Sandor ... darling, what can you mean?

TURAI. It's perfectly obvious what I mean. It is agony for an artist to discover that the fruits of his genius have been delivered into the hands of a couple of wholesale greengrocers. You are supposed to be in love with Justin Deverell, the international jewel thief who came on board at Monte Carlo. He kindled a little flame in your heart the moment you caught sight of him coming up the gangplank. The boat has now travelled south to warmer parts and so has the little flame, and you're kissing him as though he were about to turn into a frog.

IVOR. Did you call me a greengrocer?

TURAI. I did. Why do you ask?

GAL. I've known some very decent greengrocers. Of course I haven't heard them sing. Anybody care for a little chicken, ham, duck...?

TURAI. Are you still eating?

GAL. Barely. My system rejects food, as you know. I have to employ subterfuge to get anything past my lips.

TURAI. You seem to be employing a firm of caterers. What is the meaning of this picnic? Are you expecting guests?

NATASHA. Darling Alex ... I feel like a little duck...

TURAI. You sing like a little duck and *(to IVOR:)* you act like an enormous ham.

IVOR. I have never met anyone so rude.

TURAI. You have evidently never met an international jewel thief either. I see him as the sort of chap who travels and steals jewels. A bit of a Raffles if you like, and if you can manage it. Not, shall we say, the sort of chap who cuts a swathe through the lock-up garages of Canning Town.

IVOR. Who the hell do you think you are to talk to me like that?

TURAI. *(surprised and cold)* I think I am your author, a simple teller of tales and setter of scenes ... on whom your future hangs like a dead fish from a telegraph wire.

NATASHA. *(warningly) Ivor...*

TURAI. *(smiling at IVOR)* Shall we get on?

IVOR. Yes...yes...let's get on, for heavens sake. I mean we're not getting into the part which...which needs the work. *(to NATASHA:)* Are we?

NATASHA. He quite right Sandor we really ought to work on the Casablanca bit.

TURAI. Where would you like to go from?

NATASHA and IVOR. Mother is coming up for sale this afternoon.

TURAI. Excellent choice. The cruise ship Dodo has arrived at Casablanca—

GAL. *Dido* for God's sake? You're not going to name a boat after a typist's error.

TURAI. I certainly am. That woman was inspired.

GAL. She wasn't inspired. She was Polish.

TURAI. The Dodo has reached—

NATASHA. You don't have to tell us the plot - we're in it, aren't we, Ivor?

IVOR. Absolutely.

GAL. I can't follow it at all.

IVOR. But you wrote it.

GAL. That's what worries me.

TURAI. It's perfectly simple. Sir Reginald Sackville-Stew who has joined the cruise under the name of Reggie Robinsod—

GAL. Are you going to call him Robinsod?

TURAI. Look, is there anything else which doesn't meet with your approval?

GAL. The mayonnaise isn't really up to snuff.

TURAI. I'm sorry about that.

GAL. Worse things happen at sea.

TURAI. I'm trying to fix our bearings with a resume of the plot.

GAL. Do, do. I wish I could help.

TURAI. *(resuming)* Sir Reginald Sackville-Stew, for all his wealth and his famous jewel collection, has been denied happiness since his baby daughter was kidnapped from her pram some ... *(He glances speculatively at NATASHA.)* twenty-nine years ago.

NATASHA. Who is lighting me in this show? The police?

TURAI. There won't be any show if you don't keep quiet.

NATASHA. And where's my real mother, Lady Sackville-Stew?

TURAI. *(losing patience)* She died giving you a very wide birth! Leaving behind not only you and Sir Reginald but also the famous Sackville-Stew emerald ear-rings, the world's largest pair of matching emeralds, which Sir Reginald had made up into ear-clips as a parturition gift for his lovely wife.

NATASHA. Parturition gift *(emotionally)* All my mother

wanted was a decent obstetrician and you despatch her with a couple of clips on the ear!

Ivor. I see! So in fact the old dragon who's got the other ear-ring isn't Ilona's mother at all ... because Ilona is, of course, Sir Reginald's missing daughter!

Gal. So that's it!

Ivor. It's the way we keep calling mother mother. It's confusing.

Gal. Turai - I think I see it. It will be like the Chorus in Henry V.

Natasha. *(stunned)* There's a chorus in Henry V?

Gal. *(ignoring her)* The curtain rises. The Dodo at sea. Sunny day, gentle swell. Passengers disport themselves on deck. Beach ball here, cocktails there. Half-a-dozen debutantes. A girl - shy, an unspoilt beauty, simply dressed, smiling at an elegant grey-haired man, immaculate white suit. Close by, her amusingly garish mother has paused to speak to a debonair young man in a rakish yachting cap with something mocking about his eyes ... an Irish policeman appears on the poop ...

*(DVORNICHEK appears at the top of the steps with another cognac.)*

Gal. With one speech he puts us in the picture! It's Murphy.

Dvornichek. Me?

Gal. No, not you—

Dvornichek. No problem. It's like this. Ilona has won the big prize in the raffle at the charity ball, i.e. two tickets for a round-the-world cruise, donated by the Sackville-

Stew Line which owns the sister ships Dodo and Aeneas.

GAL. *(to TURAI:)* Excuse me.

TURAI. There'll be a small change there, Murphy - the sister ships Dodo and Emu.

DVORNICHEK. Much better. Well, then. Sir Reginald Sackville-Stew, spotting the lucky winner across the crowded ballroom is immediately smitten with Ilona who reminds him a little of his late wife, for very good reason though he doesn't know that yet because Ilona already has a mother as far as she's aware, and being unmarried and a bit of a wallflower until Justin Deverell takes the pins out of her hair but that's getting ahead of the story, she naturally brings mother along on the second ticket, and Sir Reginald decides to join the cruise incognito ... calling himself Reggie Robinsod, because he wants to be sure that if Ilona returns his feelings on some moonlit deck it won't be because he owns the *deck,* all clear so far? Of course, it's all going to come out with the ear-rings which Sir Reginald gave his wife - one of which went missing soon afterwards, about the same time as the Sackville-Stew baby was kidnapped, say no more for the moment, and the other of which was stolen quite recently by guess who, and given to Ilona during a duet on the poop deck; because when Reggie Robinsod recognizes the ear-ring, Justin realizes that Reggie must be Sackville-Stew, since that's who he's stolen it from, though in fact Reggie has recognized the matching one which has been in Mother's possession for all those years - which is why Mother realizes suddenly whose baby she'd stolen, everybody happy? Mind you, all this is just the sauce for the meat of the matter, which is that owing to the slump, Reg has leased out one of the sister ships to what he doesn't realize is a gang of white-slave traders supplying girls to the North African market. Unfortunately, there has been a mix up in the paper work and the Emu is at this moment full of French tarts on a round-the-world cruise while the Dodo is tied up at Casablanca.

GAL. Murphy ... have a cognac.

DVORNICHEK. Thank you sir. *(He drinks the cognac.)*

TURAI. Would it be all right if I had one too?

DVORNICHEK. Certainly, sir.

IVOR. *(stopping DVORNICHEK)* How did you know all that?

DVORNICHEK. It's in the script.

*(DVORNICHEK leaves. Rather suddenly, the Italian Castle appears to have hit rough water. DVORNICHEK who has been braced against the non-apparent swell, starts to find his feet as the others begin to lose theirs ... this happens between the end of his long speech and his exit. The onset of the storm may be indicated by whatever means possible ... including the movement of furniture, and of the visible horizon if there is one.)*

IVOR. It is?

GAL. Of course it is ... scattered about ... most of it...

NATASHA. Adam, I know how you feel darling but don't lose heart, it will be all right on the night or even sooner. *(to TURAI:)* That's what rehearsals are for, aren't they, if we can just get on.

TURAI. Very well let's get on.

GAL. Isn't it a little rough?

TURAI. Rough? It's simply under-rehearsed. Where were we?

NATASHA. Was it something about mother being for sale?

TURAI. I believe it was. Naples has fallen below the horizon. Mother has eluded the Italian police only to come to grief in Casablanca where she is in the hands of the white slavers. Ilona finds Justin on deck.

NATASHA. Justin.

IVOR. Oh Ilona.

NATASHA. Mother is coming up for sale.

*(But almost at once loud electric bells ring out. The rehearsal falters and simultaneously DVORNICHEK appears upstage and addresses everybody through a megaphone.)*

DVORNICHEK. Everybody on deck! Go to your panic stations! No lifeboats! Sorry! - Go to your lifeboat stations - no panic!

TURAI. Stay where you are!

DVORNICHEK. A to K, the starboard davits! - L to Z port beam amidships! - and don't crowd the fences!

IVOR. Are we sinking?

DVORNICHEK. I knew there was something! - get your life jackets! *(DVORNICHEK rushes out.)*

TURAI. Did I tell you to dismiss! *(to IVOR:)* Where do you think you're going?

IVOR. I can't swim! *(IVOR runs up the stairs and disappears.)*

TURAI. The utter selfishness of it! - The ingratitude!—

NATASHA. *(Who has remained calm.)* But Sandor, for all you know we *are* sinking.

TURAI. What if we are? - A boat this big can take hours to go down! Are you afraid of getting your feet wet?

*(TURAI encounters GAL who has gathered up a few necessary provisions from the buffet and is taking his leave.)*

TURAI. Et tu, Brute?

GAL. Excuse me Turai, the life rafts may be overcrowded I thought I'd book a table. *(ADAM has not moved from the piano.)*

TURAI. Like rats leaving a sinking ship. I shall complain to the captain. Where do I find him?

GAL. Try the lifeboat. *(This takes TURAI and GAL out of sight.)*

NATASHA. Adam ... ? If you're staying I'm going to stay with you. You can't get along without me. *(ADAM plays his reply, 'I Get Along Without You Very Well'.)* No, you don't. *(ADAM plays, 'I Want To Be Happy.')* And I can't be happy either till I've made you happy. *(ADAM plays, 'Goodbye.')* All right, I'll go. *(ADAM plays, 'Abide With Me.')* All right, I'll stay. I'll go down singing accompanied by Adam on the paino.

NATASHA. *(sings)*
I'LL NEVER SEE EIGHTEEN AGAIN
OR TWENTY-EIGHT OR NINE,
I'LL NEVER BE SO GREEN AGAIN
TO THINK THAT LOVE'S A VALENTINE.

ADAM.
LET'S NOT TALK IF YOU DON'T MIND
I'M NOT SURPRISED YOU LOOK SURPRISED.
IT'S NOT THAT I WANT TO BE UNKIND
BUT LOVE IS HARDER THAN I REALIZED.
NATASHA.
WHO SAID IT WOULD BE EASY?
NOT ME - YOU NEVER HEARD IT FROM ME.
WHOEVER TOLD YOU THAT LOVE WAS JUST A
     BREEZE,
SHE WAS EAGER TO PLEASE - NOT ME
YOU'LL NEVER HEAR IT FROM ME
WHO SAID IT WOULD BE COSY?
ADAM.
NOT ME - YOU NEVER HEARD IT FROM ME.
WHOEVER TOLD YOU THAT LOVE WAS LIKE A
     ROSE
HE WAS KEEN TO PROPOSE - NOT ME
YOU'LL NEVER HEAR IT FROM ME.
NATASHA.
WHO SAID IT WOULD BE EASY? - NOT ME.
ADAM.
NOT ME - YOU NEVER HEARD IT FROM ME.
NATASHA.
WHOEVER TOLD YOU THAT LOVE WAS JUST A
     BREEZE.
ADAM.
HE WAS OFF HIS TRAPEZE—
NATASHA.
NOT ME—

BOTH.
YOU'LL NEVER HEAR IT FROM ME.

*(DVORNICHEK enters, makes immediately for the telephone.)*

DVORNICHEK. He's coming. He's furious. He wants to talk to the captain.

NATASHA. Why's that, Dvornie?

DVORNICHEK. We're not sinking. *(into the telephone:)* Connect me with the captain - he's in the wardrobe.

NATASHA. Sandor is furious because we're not sinking?

DVORNICHEK. *(to telephone:)* Have it your own way, wardroom. *(to NATASHA:)* It was just a practice. Like a fire drill when it's not a boat. *(to telephone:)* Well, on the Mauretania we always called the wardroom the wardrobe. I don't know why - just get on with it - Mr. Turai wants him. *(to NATASHA:)* Good thing it was, too - turned out my job was to make sure there was no one left on board.

NATASHA. Why you?

DVORNICHEK. It's one of their traditions, apparently. Last on, last off.

*(TURAI enters and is fuming.)*

TURAI. Damn cheek!

DVORNICHEK. *(correcting him mildly)* Dvornichek.

TURAI. Have you got him?

DVORNICHEK. Nearly.

TURAI. Where's Gal? Where's Fish?

NATASHA. Sandor, stop pouting. The sea is too rough

for rehearsal anyway.

TURAI. I am about to do something about that.

NATASHA. *(alarmed)* Sandor, don't you think you ought to lie down?

DVORNICHEK. *(into phone:)* Ah! Is that you, Skip? *(TURAI snatches the receiver out of his hand.)*

TURAI. Turai! - Now look here, I haven't got time to rehearse your disasters as well as my own! Turai, Sandor Turai! Oh really, how kind of you to say so. My secret is uninterrupted rehearsal, since you ask. Oh, have you ... ? Yes, I'd adore to read it. Set on an ocean liner, eh? - What a good idea. I'll send the steward to pick it up. Actually, there is something you can do for me. As we are having such a rough crossing - Really? How interesting. Nevertheless, it is a bit rough by the standards of crossing Piccadilly, and it occurred to me that the boat may not be pointing in the best direction - we seem to be banging against the storm ... Against the swell, yes ... so if you could possibly give us an hour or two of pointing the other way ... What? - Oh, I think you'd enjoy it - I think it's very much your sort of thing ... It would be my pleasure they'll be at the box office in your name ... Absolutely - and about the other matter ... That's very decent of you. Yes, I'll hold on—

*(IVOR has entered in a bright yellow jacket which hides most of him.)*

NATASHA. You look ridiculous.

IVOR. I'm not taking it off.

NATASHA. *(to IVOR:)* I am not singing 'This Could Be The

*One'* to a man in a life jacket.

IVOR.  I thought we should just read one or two scenes -
*(a meaningful glance towards ADAM)* The sea is too rough
for anything else.

NATASHA.  Sandor is doing something about that.

TURAI.  *(into phone:)* Fine, fine - I'm most grateful, go
ahead...

IVOR.  *(labouredly amused)* Oh Yes? - Who's he talking
to? God?

*(And indeed the dangerously swaying room now rapidly calms
down.)*

TURAI.  *(into phone:)* Better ... bit more ... that's about it
... that'll do nicely ... thank you, I look forward to meeting
you too - but not just yet if you don't mind! *(TURAI
replaces the telephone, IVOR approaches it with amazement.)* He
can only give us an hour. Murphy, get me a cognac.

DVORNICHEK.  Aye, aye sir.

TURAI.  And you'd better pick up the Captain's
manuscript.

DVORNICHEK.  Aye aye.

TURAI.  By the way, when do you sleep?

DVORNICHEK.  In the winter, sir. *(DVORNICHEK
leaves.)*

TURAI.  I'm not leaving this boat without that man in
my retinue.

IVOR.  *(examining the telephone)* It's a trick, is it? *(No one
takes any notice of him.)*

TURAI.  Where's Gal?

*(GAL enters with a tiny snack, removing a life jacket.)*

GAL. *(feelingly)* The women and children on this boat don't give an inch.

TURAI. *(to IVOR:)* Take off that absurd article. If we hit an iceberg. I will arrange for you to be informed. *(IVOR with ill grace removes himself from the lifejacket. Meanwhile NATASHA has carried a tray of delicate sandwiches to ADAM.)*

NATASHA. Adam, darling, why don't you eat some thing - you mustn't be so minor key.

TURAI. Leave him alone. I want him to save his voice *(to ADAM:)* Me fortissimo, you piano.

NATASHA. *(losing her temper)* Shut up! I've had quite enough of you!

IVOR. So have I. And if we hit an iceberg I would con-sider it an improvement on the present situation, especially if you go down with the ship.

TURAI. *(calmly)* So. It seems that my legendary good nature towards petulant children, rabid dogs and actors as a class, coupled with my detestation of sarcasm and mockery in all its forms, especially when directed at the mentally disabled, has lulled you into impudence and given you a misplaced air of indispensibility, what I like to call a sine-qua-nonchalance. I am to blame for this. I have mollycoddled you. I have made obeisance to your exiguous talent. I have forborne to point out the distance that separates your performance from an adequate realization of the character I have created for you. That there is such a distance you may have no doubt. I myself have just sent out for a pair of bifocals, and I'm thinking of borrowing the captain's telescope.

NATASHA. *(with dignity)* I'm sorry if I do not seem to suit your little play. It requires a large adjustment for someone connected, as I am, with the Shakespearean theatre.

TURAI. If you are referring to your Juliet, you might as well claim a connection with the Orient Express by virtue of having once been derailed at East Finchley.

NATASHA. *(leaving)* Rrright. If you require to speak to me you will find me in my cabin.

TURAI. *(pointedly)* If I require to speak to you I can make myself heard quite easily from my own.

IVOR. *(hurriedly)* No, no - let's not quarrel, eh, - I'm sorry, Turai - Natasha is sorry too - We really would like to get on *(to NATASHA:)* Wouldn't we?

NATASHA. *(collecting herself)* Yes. Let's get on.

TURAI. *(cheerfully)* That's the spirit. Darling. Dearest Natasha. Let me see a smile. No, a smile. That's better. Now I forgive you. Are we friends?

NATASHA. *(grimly)* Darling, Sandor...dearest ... we are in your hands.

TURAI. *(gallantly)* It's a privilege. And for me too. My angel. Forgive me also. I spoke in anger. I didn't mean it about your Juliet. It was right up there with your Pauline. Now where were we?

IVOR. Mother is coming up for sale this afternoon.

*(DVORNICHEK enters smartly with Captain's manuscript and cognac on a tray.)*

DVORNICHEK. Here we are sir. One cognac and one copy of '*All In The Same Boat*' with the captains's compliments.

TURAI. About time! Over here and take that rubbish away. I'd like your opinion of it.

DVORNICHEK. Right. *(DVORNICHEK hands TURAI the manuscript and drinks the cognac.)* I've had better. Will there be anything else sir?

TURAI. A cognac.

DVORNICHEK. Certainly sir.

NATASHA. *(shouts)* Mother is coming up for sale this afternoon.

IVOR. *(in character)* I know all about it. Reggie is with the radio officer trying to contact the Emu.

NATASHA. The Emir?

IVOR. No, no, there's been a mix up with the sister ships. The Emu has reached Athens and the girls who were supposed to be delivered to the Casbah cash in advance are running around taking pictures of the Acropolis.

NATASHA. Oh Justin.

IVOR. I can't see any problem. Your mother is for sale. I will buy her. There's only one thing I need from you, Ilona.

NATASHA. Of course! *(She mimes removing an earring and giving it to IVOR.)*

IVOR. So it's farewell to the Sackville-Stew emeralds. *(This, of course, for ADAM'S benefit ... but, unfortunately, ADAM has now eaten his way towards a revelation of the engraving upon the silver tray, underneath the sandwiches. The engraving, naturally, is familiar to him. He starts to catch on ... and begins to investigate the other silver salvers, emptying them of their contents one by one, until he has a collection of perhaps half a dozen trays identical to the one TURAI had presented to him. He has approached TURAI with these trays and now reproachfully hands them to him - after which ADAM leaves the stage. GAL has noticed all this, and with an anxious glance at TURAI, GAL hurriedly follows ADAM off the stage. NATASHA and IVOR have remained unware of their departure.)*

TURAI. All right, there's no point in going on with that.

IVOR. *(seizing his opportunity)* I'm afraid you're right Turai - but don't worry. While you were in Deauville I thought I'd pen to paper, don't you know, and - erm - Natasha and I have something to show you.

TURAI. *(gravely)* I am inexpressively touched.

IVOR. Thank you. It's probably no good.

TURAI. Come, come, I'd be privileged to be given a glimpse.

IVOR. Well, it's the bit which starts off with mother coming up for sale - we've rehearsed and rehearsed ... *(Meanwhile NATASHA, after a couple of sidelong glances, has missed Adam...)*

NATASHA. Ivor...

IVOR. *(heedlessly)* You know, getting it right for you, almost to the last minute - I think you will find it quite moving—

TURAI. Indeed. What a shame Adam isn't here to see it.

IVOR. Yes, isn't it - What? *(He looks around.)* Damn and blast it! *(GAL hurries back into the room.)*

GAL. He's not in his room. He seemed upset about something. *(drily)* I see you have recovered some of the family silver. These shipping lines are completely unscrupulous.

*(DVORNICHEK enters with a cognac on the usual silver tray.)*

DVORNICHEK. Here we are sir! One cognac. *(TURAI, who is already carrying several silver trays furiously grabs DVORNICHEK's tray while DVORNICHEK deftly saves the glass of cognac.)*

TURAI. Will you stop filling this room with these damned trays!

DVORNICHEK. What am I supposed to do with the drink?

TURAI. Surely you can manage a glass of cornac?! *(DVORNICHEK downs the cognac, remarking...)*

DVORNICHEK. Oh - thank you very much. Good health. Will there be anything else?

TURAI. *(with great self-control)* Have you seen Mr. Adam?

DVORNICHEK. Yes, sir - don't worry, it's all taken care of, no problem.

TURAI. What isn't?

DVORNICHEK. I gave him the telegram.

TURAI. What are you talking about?

DVORNICHEK. The telegram from his mother.

TURAI. I know you did. I was there.

DVORNICHEK. I mean the second telegram.

TURAI. Second telegram?

DVORNICHEK. Now you're getting it.

TURAI. What did it say?

DVORNICHEK. She just missed him in Cherbourg and is taking the next boat to New York.

TURAI. I'm going to faint.

DVORNICHEK. I'll get some brandy.

TURAI. Don't bother I'll throw myself overboard. *(TURAI hands the Captain's manuscript back to DVORNICHEK. TURAI and DVORNICHEK leave in opposite directions.*

GAL. Well, shall we get on?

IVOR. What for?

GAL. What for? I thought we were rehearsing.

IVOR. Oh yes.

GAL. Where were we? ... Mother is coming up for...

IVOR and NATASHA. No - no.

GAL. What's the matter?

IVOR and NATASHA. Nothing, nothing.

GAL. Perhaps we'd better go from the beginning, I'll set the scene, the curtain rises, the Dodo at sea.

NATASHA. Oh my God.

GAL. Sunny day gentle swell passengers disport themselves on deck. A girl, shy, unspoilt beauty simply dressed ... A debonair young man in a rakish yachting cap ... An Irish policeman appears on the poop.

*(TURAI staggers back on, half carrying ADAM who is wrapped in a blanket.)*

IVOR. *(baffled)* Is this right?

NATASHA. My God!

GAL. Stand back ... put him in the chair.

NATASHA. What happened?

GAL. Get some soup!

TURAI. He's all right - he jumped into the sea.

NATASHA. Adam darling, you're all wet - I'm sorry - I can explain it to you.

GAL. He must know why he's wet.

TURAI. Stop making such a fuss. He's come to no harm at all.

NATASHA. But who saved him?

*(DVORNICHEK enters wearing a bathing suit. His hair is wet, he carries a cognac on a tray, and ADAM's dripping hat, a boater.)*

DVORNICHEK. Here we are sir! One cognac.

TURAI. At last.

NATASHA. Dvornie!

DVORNICHEK. No problem. *(TURAI reaches for the cognac but NATASHA intercepts it and starts feeding it to ADAM.)*

NATASHA. Darling...

GAL. Shouldn't we take him to his cabin?

TURAI. We can't rehearse in his cabin, we'd never get the piano in there for a start.

NATASHA. For God's sake, Sandor—

TURAI. For his and for mine and not least for yours, stop pouting and pick up your cue.

GAL. Are you serious?

TURAI. It has been a day of constant and frivolous interruptions. I am not prepared to indulge any of you anymore. It's the January sale at the slave market and Mother is lot one. Ilona tells Justin the bad news but Justin has a plan, carry on...

NATASHA. He's right! *(to IVOR, shouts:)* Mother is coming up for sale this afternoon, and you can't see any problem!

IVOR. *(taking the hint)* I can't see any problem! Your mother is for sale! I will buy her.

NATASHA. Justin!...

DVORNICHEK. Gerald.

NATASHA. Gerald.

IVOR. There's only one thing I need from you Ilona.

NATASHA. Of course!

IVOR. So it's farewell to the Sackville-Stew emeralds. It's funny how little they mean to me now. It is I who have been robbed, for you have stolen my heart... *(sings)* "You stole my heart and made an honest man of me".

TURAI. I can't bear it. Murphy, get me a cognac.

DVORNICHEK. Yes, sir.

TURAI. Bring the bottle, have one yourself.

DVORNICHEK. *(leaving)* Thank you, sir. Two bottles of cognac.

TURAI. Stock characters, stock situations, stock economy of expression. What seemed to be delightful and ingenious like a chiming pocket watch, turns out to be a clanking medieval town hall clock where nothing happens for fifteen minutes and then a couple of stiff figures trundle into view and hit a cracked bell with a hammer - bonk! - Justin is a jewel thief! Bonk! Reggie is Sir Reginald! Bonk! Predictable from top to bottom.

IVOR. I think it's just the last part, really.

TURAI. Bonk! Jewel thief reformed by love of good

woman! Bonk! They win the mixed doubles at ping-pong! *(This is IVOR'S big moment.)*

IVOR. Excuse me Turai. I think I might be able to help you on this one.

TURAI. Oh really?

IVOR. Yes. The fact is that while you three were in Deauville, Natasha and I were in talking about the ending and we thought it was a bit bonk bonk, don't you know?

TURAI. *(coldly)* I beg your pardon?

IVOR. Well, we did. A bit predictable, we thought *(to NATASHA:)* Didn't we?

NATASHA. Yes. Sort of bonk ... bonk.

TURAI. Bonk bonk?

IVOR. Yes. Well, as you know, I have a certain gift for, well, words, really.

TURAI. How would I know that since you have always gone to such trouble to conceal it?

NATASHA. Not so much words as construction.

IVOR. That's it - I tell wonderful stories.

TURAI. *(incredulously)* To whom?

NATASHA. *(snaps)* Let him finish, Sandor!

IVOR. Well, the long and the short of it is that I thought I'd put pen to paper and Natasha and I have worked up a little scene if you'd like us to do it for you. All right?

TURAI. In all my born days I have never encountered such brass. I have had actors who won't take their trousers off, I have had actors who won't work with cats or in the provinces, in short I have had from actors every kind of interference with the artistic process but I have never had an actor with the effrontery to write.

IVOR. I say, look here Turai—

TURAI. The nerve of it!

NATASHA. *(finally)* Sandor!

TURAI. What, pray, is the burden of your little scene?

IVOR. I suppose you could say it was less bonk bonk... and more hiccup.

TURAI. Hiccup?

IVOR. Yes. One more boy-loses-girl before boy-gets-girl.

GAL. *(interested)* How do you achieve that?

NATASHA. Ilona agrees to marry Reggie, then when they announce their engagement, Mother has hysterics because she can't marry her own father and the truth comes out so Ilona is free to marry Justin after all, I thought it was rather clever, actually. Well done, Ivor.

TURAI. Gal, have you ever heard anything like it?

GAL. Yes, but let's not dismiss it on that account *(to NATASHA:)* Where do we go from?

IVOR and NATASHA. 'Mother is coming up for sale this afternoon.' *(NATASHA and IVOR resume their characters.)*

IVOR. I know, it's rotten luck. At least no one is likely to buy her.

NATASHA. That's just where you're wrong. Reggie is going to buy her.

IVOR. Reggie! That's disgusting! To think that an Englishman—

NATASHA. No, no he's buying her for me!

IVOR. Oh I see.

NATASHA. You know what this means Justin?

IVOR. We'll have your mother around again.

NATASHA. Apart from that. I have told Reggie that I will marry him.

IVOR. What?

NATASHA. I must. It's a matter of honour.

IVOR. I will outbid him!

NATASHA. With what?

IVOR. You're right, Ilona. I have never put anything aside for the future, not a single cufflink. Wait! - It's not too late! I have stolen the ear-ring twice, I can steal it again!

NATASHA. It is too late. Look - *(She sweeps back her lovely hair, both sides.)* my engagement present from Reggie!

IVOR. The Sackville-Stew pearls!

GAL. Emeralds.

IVOR. I've made it pearls.

GAL. Why?

IVOR. Well—

NATASHA. A pearl is much better - babies are always swallowing them.

GAL. But it was in your little fist.

NATASHA. No, it was in my little potty.

GAL. You said it was obscene.

NATASHA. An emerald would be obscene. A pearl is perfectly sweet. *(resuming)* Goodbye, Justin.

IVOR. Let me kiss you one last time my darling. *(ADAM has been slowly coming to life and taking an interest. But, having done so, he has lost interest. He has decided to leave. He begins to depart in an exhausted kind of way, and it seems that he might go out of earshot before the critical part of the scene arrives ... but noticing him going, IVOR and NATASHA forge ahead resolutely, and as ADAM begins to recognize the words he halts.)*

NATASHA. Just this once. Don't get carried away.

IVOR. My angel!

NATASHA. Now, you promised not to get carried away.

IVOR. I can't help it!

NATASHA. You're not going to begin again!

IVOR. Yes, again! And again! I love you, I adore you, I worship you! I worship you as the moth worships the candle flame! I love you as the Eiffel Tower loves the little fleecy cloud that dances around it in the summer breeze ... *(GAL and ADAM have turned to look at each other in amazement.)*

NATASHA. You'll soon forget me!

GAL. Excuse me ... What was that he said?

NATASHA. Please don't interrupt *(resuming)* You'll soon forget me.

IVOR. No, no I'm mad about you! But you've plucked out my heart like the olive out of a dry martini and dashed me from your lips!

NATASHA. Don't spoil everything we've had together.

GAL. *(to TURAI:)* Excuse me Turai.

TURAI. What is it?

NATASHA. Come, give me your hands.

GAL. We've heard this before.

NATASHA. I will remember your hands—

TURAI. I thought it seemed familiar.

NATASHA. Such clever wicked hands too when I think of what they have done.

TURAI. Who's he got it from? Sardou?

GAL. No, we heard it last night!

TURAI. Of course!

IVOR. What's going on? This isn't fair to my work.

NATASHA. Please be a good boy. Remember this afternoon. Here, let me kiss you.

IVOR. That's not a kiss, that's a tip. Let the whole world know I'm a dashed Martini!

NATASHA. That's not true. You will always be the first. If I had ten husbands, no one can take your place, but I'm engaged to be married so please be kind and leave me now.

IVOR. All right, I will. Only let me see you as I want to remember you. Lift your hair. Let me move your collar just a little—

NATASHA. Oh, you're impossible - what are you doing?

IVOR. One last look - one touch - I beg you! Oh that pink round perfection! Let me put my lips to its rose smoothness.

GAL. Her ear-ring!

IVOR. And the other one!

GAL. Her other ear-ring!

IVOR. How beautifully they hang there!

TURAI. Enough!

ADAM. Natasha!

TURAI. This is revolting!

IVOR. What did you think in general?

TURAI. It won't do.

ADAM. *(without pause)* Yes, it will. It will do wonderfully!

TURAI. You thought it good?

ADAM. *(without pause)* I thought it the best play I've ever seen.

NATASHA. *(realizing)* Adam—

ADAM. *(to NATASHA:)* You were wonderful. I've never liked you better or loved you more.

GAL. *(realizing)* I say, Adam, my boy—

ADAM. *(gaily)* Don't Adam-my-boy me - in my opinion Ivor knocks Gal and Turai and Shakespeare into a cocked heap.

TURAI. *(realizing)* How extraordinary!

ADAM. Ivor, let me shake you by the hand.

IVOR. How do you do? We've never really said hello.

ADAM. Hello, hello, hello.

NATASHA. Adam! You're speaking!

ADAM. Of course I am!

NATASHA. You're cured! *(ADAM hesitates, realizing.)*

ADAM. Good heavens. *(pause)* So I am.

NATASHA. Don't stop! I love you. *(pause)* Adam? *(ADAM pauses but he is teasing.)*

ADAM. *(rapidly)* I love you, I love you, I love you. Ask me a question - quick - any question.

NATASHA. Will you marry me?

ADAM. *(instantly)* Without hesitation, because I love you, I love you, I love you.

*(DVORNICHEK with a cognac glass and a bottle on a tray has walked in on this. He approaches TURAI.)*

DVORNICHEK. Here we are sir - one cognac. *(ADAM snatches the bottle and glass.)*

ADAM. Thank you Dvornichek. I love you too! I love everybody! *(He fills the glass and unexpectedly hands it to*

*TURAI, TURAI takes it gravely.)* Your cognac.

TURAI. At last. *(and drinks it)*

*(The telephone rings - ADAM picks up the telephone.)*

ADAM. *(into telephone:)* Yes? Adam Adam here, the conversationalist ... Hello, captain! Art thou sleeping there below? ... Hang on, I'll ask him *(to TURAI:)* Have you had a chance to look through *'All In The Same Boat'?*

TURAI. I will have to ask my literary consultant.

DVORNICHEK. Hopeless.

TURAI. Hopeless.

ADAM. *(into the telephone:)* Hopeless. *(ADAM hangs up.)* He seemed upset.

*(The ships HOOTER sounds. A moment later the boat shudders and everything starts to sway again as the boat moves back into the wrong direction.)*

TURAI. Some people can't take constructive criticism.

DVORNICHEK. Early praise isn't good for them. Let them struggle, otherwise they'll never strive for perfection - writing, rewriting, up to the last minute.

TURAI. Quite - get me a cognac.

DVORNICHEK. You've got one in your hand. Burning the midnight oil.

TURAI. I want two cognacs.

DVORNICHEK. The bottle's there. Writing through the night.

ADAM. *(to DVORNICHEK:)* What was that?

DVORNICHEK. What was what?

ADAM. Mr. Turai was up writing through the night?

DVORNICHEK. *(pause)* Problem!

ADAM. What a fool I've been. *(to IVOR:)* Ivor, did you write that scene while we were in Deauville? I asked you a question. Did you write that scene?

NATASHA. Of course he did! Answer him, Ivor!

GAL. He can't speak. He's got Adam's disease. *(He has.)*

ADAM. *(to TURAI:)* I owe you everything, you and Mr. Gal. You are my benefactors, my friends. I know that you won't lie to me.

TURAI. And you are quite right. I am incapable of lying to you. You are like a son to me. You are more. You are youth, idealism. You are the future. To lie to you would be a crime.

ADAM. Did Ivor write that scene?

TURAI. Every word.

GAL. Thank God.

NATASHA. You see!

ADAM. *(not celebrating yet)* Then I have one more question.

TURAI. You wish to know, in that case, what was I working on last night?

ADAM. Yes.

TURAI. I will tell you exactly. Last night I realized we were on the wrong boat.

GAL. To New York?

TURAI. To Casablanca. You are right about the ending, you are right about the beginning, and the middle is unspeakable. I have spent the day in an agony of indecision but now my mind is made up. The Dodo is a dud and we have to scuttle her here and now.

GAL. But we're contracted to arrive in New York with—

TURAI. A much better story is staring us in the face.

GAL. What's that?

TURAI. 'The Cruise of the Emu'.

DVORNICHEK. Much better.

ADAM. Oh, thank God!

TURAI. I thought you'd like it.

ADAM. No, no I mean - oh, fogive me!

NATASHA. Adam, what is all this about?

ADAM. Nothing, a storm in a teapot! I love you all over again! He was writing the cruise of the other thing!

GAL. Well, we've got four days. Where do we start?

TURAI. Well...

GAL. I know - with Murphy!

DVORNICHEK. Me. sir?

GAL. No, actually, I meant...

DVORNICHEK. No problem. It's like this. The Emu under the command of a handsome young captain, who is unaware that on board there is a beautiful stowaway who, unbeknownst to him and to her, is a missing heiress, is circumnavigating the globe with a full complement of French tarts, who are ignorant of the fact that the white slavers, little knowing that there has been a mix up with the sister ships, intend to take over the boat with Pepe the Silent.

TURAI. Who the hell is Pepe the Silent?

DVORNICHEK. *(indicating IVOR)* The white slavers' ugly henchman who's had his tongue cut out and is silently in love with the missing heiress, so saves her life and remains silent while she goes off with the man she loves; very moving, usually.

TURAI. Fish, you're a lucky man. How did you know all that?

DVORNICHEK. It's the captain's manuscript, sir.

TURAI. It is?

DVORNICHEK. He can't write but he has a certain gift for construction and absolutely no original ideas of any kind.

TURAI. He sounds like a natural. Adam, you've got the part.

ADAM. Who'll play the piano?

TURAI. Murphy?

DVORNICHEK. I'm a bit rusty.

TURAI. Serves you right for getting wet. Can you read music?

DVORNICHEK. No problem.

TURAI. Murphy, have a cognac.

DVORNICHEK. Thank you, sir, and may I say what a pleasure it is to serve you, sir - you are, if I may say so, sir, quite a swell. *(DVORNICHEK takes command of the piano. NATASHA and ADAM go into the song.)*

NATASHA.

WHEN I SAW YOU...

ADAM.

MY KNEES WENT WEAK, MY THROAT WENT DRY,

I COULD HARDLY SPEAK.

BOTH.

ISN'T IT HEAVENLY!

—THIS COULD BE THE ONE.

GLORY BE WHEN YOU KISSED ME,
WEDDING BELLS RANG TWO FOR TEA.
WHEN ALL'S SAID AND DONE.
THIS COULD BE THE ONE.
    TURAI. Now you kiss her. *(They kiss.)*

*(Which is the end ... but, perhaps by way of a curtain call, DVORINCHEK at the piano leads the COMPANY into...)*

    *'Where Do We Go From Here?'*

WE JUST SAID HELLO AND NOW IT'S GOODBYE
SO MIND HOW YOU GO, WE HOPE IT KEEPS
   DRY,
AND PLEASE EXCUSE MY TEAR
BUT WHERE DO WE GO FROM HERE?

WE'LL JUST CATCH THE TIDE,
IT'S ANCHORS AWEIGH,
SO THANKS FOR THE RIDE,
AND HAVE A NICE DAY
WE HAVE TO DISAPPEAR—
BUT WHERE DO WE GO FROM HERE?

THIS WAY, THAT WAY, UP OR DOWN,
WE COULD GO BOTH WAYS.
FORWARDS, BACKWARDS, ROUND AND ROUND,
WHAT DO I CARE
SO LONG AS WHEN WE GET TOGETHER,
AND WE'RE SAT BY THE FIRE
CANOODLING AND THEN

YOU FEEL THE DESIRE
TO GO ROUND AGAIN.
YOU HAVE A VOLUNTEER
SO WHERE DO WE GO FROM HERE?

SO WHERE DO WE GO—
WHEN DO WE GO—
DARLING I'M SO READY TO GO—
SO WHY DON'T WE GO FROM HERE?

# About
# TOM STOPPARD

Tom Stoppard was introduced to American audiences in 1967 with *Rosencrantz and Guildenstern Are Dead*, which was followed to Broadway by *The Real Inspector Hound*, *Jumpers*, *Travesties*, *Dirty Linen*, *Newfound-Land*, *Night and Day*, *The Real Thing*, and *Artist Descending a Staircase*. There have also been Off Broadway productions of his first play, *Enter A Free Man* and of *Dogg's Hamlet/Cahoot's Macbeth*. His other work includes translations of Arthur Schnitzer's *Undiscovered Country* and *On the Razzle* (for the National Theatre of Great Britain); *Every Good Boy Deserves Favour*, a play for actors and orchestra written with Andre Previn (which was performed at Lincoln Center); and a TV play, "Professional Foul" (also seen on PBS). He has written screenplays of *Despair*, (directed by Rainier Fassbinder), *The Human Factor*, (directed by Otto Preminger), *Brazil*, *Empire of the Sun* (directed by Steven Spielberg) and *The Russian House* (directed by Fred Schepesi). His most recent work filmed for TV is "Squaring the Circle", an "imaginary documentary" about Polish Solidarity.

Tom Stoppard lives near London with his wife, writer and broadcaster Dr. Miriam Stoppard and four sons: Oliver, Barnaby, William and Edmund.

# Also By

# Tom Stoppard

ANOTHER MOON CALLED EARTH
ARCADIA
ARTIST DESCENDING A STAIRCASE
DALLIANCE
DIRTY LINEN & NEW-FOUND-LAND
THE DISSOLUTION OF DOMINIC BOOT
THE DOG IT WAS THAT DIED
DOGG'S HAMLET, CAHOOT'S MACBETH
ENTER A FREE MAN
HAPGOOD
JUMPERS
NEUTRAL GROUND
NIGHT AND DAY
ON THE RAZZLE
THE REAL INSPECTOR HOUND
THE REAL THING
ROSENCRANTZ & GUILDENSTERN ARE DEAD
A SEPARATE PEACE
TEETH
TRAVESTIES
UNDISCOVERED COUNTRY (translation)
WHERE ARE THEY NOW?

Please visit our website **samuelfrench.com** for complete
descriptions and licensing information

# OTHER TITLES AVAILABLE FROM SAMUEL FRENCH

## HAPGOOD
Tom Stoppard

*Thriller / 8m, 1f / Interiors, Exteriors*

Does light come in waves or particles? Experiments will show either: the experimenter can choose. "A double agent is like a trick of the light," Kerner the physicist tells Blair the spy catcher. "You get what you interrogate for." Dual natures, of light and of people, are the theme of Tom Stoppard's espionage thriller. Kerner's secret research is being leaked to Moscow. Is Ridley the double? Or is Kerner a triple? Hapgood is the person to find out, and maybe it will need two of her.

"Intriguing and thoroughly absorbing."
– *London Broadcasting*

"Vastly entertaining."
– *Jewish Chronicle*

"Stoppard's most cunning play yet."
– *Guardian*

## ROSENCRANTZ & GUILDENSTERN ARE DEAD
Tom Stoppard

*Comedy / 14m, 5f, 12 extras, 6 musicians / Unit Set*

Winner of both the Tony and NY Drama Critics Circle awards. Rosencrantz and Guildenstern are the college chums of Hamlet, and their story is what happened behind the scenes in Shakespeare's play. What were they doing there in Elsinore anyway? "I don't know; we were sent for." They are not only anti agents, but also anti sympathy, anti identification, and in fact anti persons, which is uniquely demonstrated by their having such a hard time recollecting which of them goes by what name. The Players come and go; Prince Hamlet comes through reading words, words, words; foul deeds are done; Hamlet is sent abroad, escapes death; and in turn Rosencrantz and Guildenstern find their "only exit is death."

"Very funny, very brilliant, very chilling; it has the dust of
thought about it and the particles glitter excitingly in the
theatrical air."
- *The New York Times*

"A stimulating, funny, imaginative comedy."
- *New York Daily News*

## MURDER AMONG FRIENDS
Bob Barry

*Comedy Thriller / 4m, 2f / Interior*
Take an aging, exceedingly vain actor; his very rich wife; a double dealing, double loving agent, plunk them down in an elegant New York duplex and add dialogue crackling with wit and laughs, and you have the basic elements for an evening of pure, sophisticated entertainment. Angela, the wife and Ted, the agent, are lovers and plan to murder Palmer, the actor, during a contrived robbery on New Year's Eve. But actor and agent are also lovers and have an identical plan to do in the wife. A murder occurs, but not one of the planned ones.

"Clever, amusing, and very surprising."
– *New York Times*

"A slick, sophisticated show that is modern and very funny."
– WABC TV

OTHER TITLES AVAILABLE FROM SAMUEL FRENCH

## THE RIVERS AND RAVINES
Heather McDonald

*Drama / 9m, 5f / Unit Set*
Originally produced to acclaim by Washington D.C.'s famed
Arena Stage. This is an engrossing political drama about the
contemporary farm crisis in America and its effect on rural
communities.

"A haunting and emotionally draining play. A community of
farmers and ranchers in a small Colorado town disintegrates
under the weight of failure and thwarted ambitions. Most of
the farmers, their spouses, children, clergyman, banker and
greasy spoon proprietress survive, but it is survival without
triumph. This is an *Our Town* for the 80's."
– *The Washington Post*

OTHER TITLES AVAILABLE FROM SAMUEL FRENCH

## THE DECORATOR
Donald Churchill

*Comedy / 1m, 2f / Interior*
Marcia returns to her flat to find it has not been painted as she arranged. A part time painter who is filling in for an ill colleague is just beginning the work when the wife of the man with whom Marcia is having an affair arrives to tell all to Marcia's husband. Marcia hires the painter a part time actor to impersonate her husband at the confrontation. Hilarity is piled upon hilarity as the painter, who takes his acting very seriously, portrays the absent husband. The wronged wife decides that the best revenge is to sleep with Marcia's husband, an ecstatic experience for them both. When Marcia learns that the painter/actor has slept with her rival, she demands the opportunity to show him what really good sex is.

"Irresistible."
– *London Daily Telegraph*

"This play will leave you rolling in the aisles....
I all but fell from my seat laughing."
– *London Star*

CPSIA information can be obtained at www.ICGtesting.com
Printed in the USA
LVOW012128280911

248365LV00007B/3/P